Heaven's
Ridge

David Lewis Paget

BARR BOOKS

For my wife, Lyn…
Who would have all my characters
ride off happily into the sunset…

Sorry!

Set in 14pt Times New Roman

The characters in this novel are mainly fictitious.
The actions ascribed to the two historic characters,
Cecil Rhodes and Barney Barnato, are fictitious.
Any similarity between the other characters in
this book and persons living or dead is purely
coincidental.

ISBN – 978-0-9596876-1-3

Chapter One

Ingrid Schuman sat bolt upright on her stool at the bar of the Gold Ridge Hotel, and sipped her sherry. She was alone in the bar, as she'd known she would be. It was Monday morning, and the only other sign of activity was the manager, appearing every now and then from his other duties to fill up her glass. After the third refill, he cleared his throat.

'Don't you think you should be getting on home, Miss Ingrid? Your sister won't be too happy if she finds you out like this.'

Ingrid stared straight ahead, and pursed her lips. The wine was beginning to go to her head, and the severity of her frown was tempered now by a glassiness around the eyes.

'Don't you worry about me, Evans. I can look after myself!'

She took another tiny sip, and straightened her head and shoulders as if in self-assertion. She was the picture of an old-time spinster, though not unattractive. She was small of stature, with creases of disappointment around her eyes. She had the overall aspect of one who is constantly saddened by life's reluctance to provide a renewable source of happiness.

Her look might have been softened had she worn her hair down, but it was brushed tightly back and contained in a bun at her neck She wore a black gown, very old-fashioned and staid, with a brooch at the breast and a small gold necklace. Although she was forty two years of age, she could have passed for thirty-five given the influence of a hair stylist and half-decent couturier.

Ingrid had lived at Heaven's Ridge all her life, and no event in her life had ever provided the impetus for her to want to leave. Her great-great-grandfather had built this Hotel some time after his return from the goldfields of Bendigo. He had decided to use his wealth to ensure that he would never again have to travel any distance for a drink. The Hotel still belonged to the family, though it had been leased out now for over eighty years.

There were never more than twenty patrons there at any one time as the local population was a sparse one, mainly travellers and prospectors. It was not exactly on a well-beaten track.

The only other retailer in this tiny cluster of buildings was a small delicatessen, which mainly dealt in milk, bread, cut meats and soft drinks. Then there were three cottages, a wooden church and a farm implements dealer, who also acted as the local mechanic, fixing cars, trucks and the odd tractor. Further up the road, off behind a tangle of hedge and stringy eucalypts, and at the end of an fifty-yard driveway, lay Heaven's Ridge.

Heaven's Ridge was the house that Theodore Schuman had built with the first fruits of his fortune, sweated out of the mining leases at Bendigo and Lambing Flat. He'd been one of the relatively few immigrants who had actually found gold, and managed to hang onto it. Later, hearing about strikes in South Australia, he'd travelled over the border and headed north, to that inhospitable country in the north of the state. He'd found nothing there to his liking, and it was only later, while travelling south again that he had stopped to camp at the site of Heaven's Ridge. It was while hammering in his tent poles there that he had struck something solid, and on investigation had discovered a ridge of gold running just under the surface and down into the ground.

The ridge was part of an escarpment that had once formed the cliffs of a sea vista, but the sea had since receded the best part of a thousand miles, and now the house looked down on a long, deserted beach, far from anywhere. In between were low sandhills and a scrubby saltbush, a hundred feet below. The view was quite breathtaking on that side. In the other direction lay the pub.

Pegging out his claim, Theodore had removed what gold was easily accessible, and headed off to Adelaide to register his claim. Within a year he was one of the wealthiest men in the state, and commissioned Heaven's Ridge, the house, to be built squarely over the top of his original find. It was said that even today, the mine was accessible from the cellar of the old house, but as no one had access to the house, this was only conjecture.

Ingrid placed her glass firmly on the bar, and flicked the rim with her finger so that it gave out a chime. Evans struggled up from the cellar, looking worried. He looked at Ingrid, then at her glass, and slowly shook his head.

'You'll get me in all sorts of trouble, Miss Ingrid,' he said. 'I really think you've had enough for today.'

The lady's face adopted a grim expression. She snorted, and rapped her fingers on the bar.

'Another one, if you please, Evans! If my sister has anything to say, just refer her to me.'

Evans looked imploringly at the ceiling, but nevertheless filled Ingrid's glass. There would be hell to pay over this, he knew, but what could you do? She was one of the owners, and as such was his landlord. What little alcoholic requirements the two ladies had were always provided gratis by the lessee.

At that moment a young man of about thirty wandered into the bar. Ingrid looked at him as if he were an intruder, then ignored him and continued sipping her drink.

'Say, landlord. Could I have a Port o' Gaff, please,' he enquired.

Evans obliged him with a schooner of the dark liquid, and took his money. As he handed him his change, he said, 'Do you intend staying on, Mister Blood, or will you be leaving today?'

The young man took a sip of his drink before replying.

'I think I'll be staying for a few days. My car's in the shop next door, being fixed – I blew the radiator last night! The guy says that the clutch fan's seized as well, which is what probably caused it. So he has to wait for the parts. I think you can say that I'll be here until the weekend, maybe longer.'

Evans wiped along the bar with a cloth.

'That's too bad. There's not really too much to see around Heaven's Ridge.'

Ingrid looked curiously at the young man, and put her drink down.

'Did I understand you to say you were at a loose end for a few days, young man?'

Graham Blood looked up, and noticed her for the first time.

'That's correct. I'm sorry, you are...?'

'My name is Ingrid Schuman. I live up the road, at Heaven's Ridge.'

'I'm Graham Blood. Pleased to meet you, I'm sure.'

He held out his hand.

Ingrid gingerly held her hand out, and allowed him to hold it by just the tip of her fingers. She suppressed a shiver as she did so. She wasn't used to shaking hands with brash young men.

'Heaven's Ridge! So that's the name of a house, as well as the place?' Graham looked interested.

'Yes. The village, if you can call it that, was named after the house. My great-great grandfather was the first to settle the area. He built the house, and he built the Hotel. He was a gold prospector, you see. And where the house is now, is where he struck gold. He'd already made his fortune, of course, at Lambing Flat, and then at Bendigo.'

Graham nodded. 'Fascinating,' he said.

'Anyway, it just struck me that if you were at all handy at fixing things, I could offer you some days of employment over at the house. It's many years since we had a man around the place, and to be frank, there are a lot of things that need fixing.'

She looked sternly at him over the rim of her glass. Graham suppressed a smile.

'That sounds like a good offer to me. I'm pretty handy with a hammer and nails. I'll only be kicking my heels otherwise, so I accept your offer. Thank you!'

Ingrid tossed her head, as she imagined a grand dame might do.

'Very well then, Mister Blood. I expect you to report over at the house at, shall we say, one o'clock.'

'That'll be fine,' he smiled, and went back to his drink.

Looking around, he picked out a small table in the corner, sat himself down and unrolled a newspaper. He was deep into the sports section when someone else entered the bar, another middle-aged lady, obviously the sister of the lady at the bar.

'So there you are! I've been looking for you everywhere!'

The newcomer's tone was angry and peevish. She was dressed in a cotton print dress edged with brocade, and looked considerably older than her sister, though in fact she was only forty eight. She was taller, thinner and more severe than the woman at the bar. She was not in the best of moods, and seeing her sister at the bar had the effect of making her more than usually astringent.

Ingrid jumped when she heard her voice, looked around, and then composed herself and turned back to the bar.

'It's you, Margaret! You made me jump! I wish you wouldn't go around making such a song and dance.'

'Back to your old tricks, eh, Ingrid? Slinking away and paying court to the demon drink!'

Ingrid laughed, sardonically.

'How melodramatic you are, Margaret. Anyone would think that I was a cupboard drinker! I merely wished to have a sherry to calm my nerves this morning, and that's what I'm having.'

Margaret went over to the bar and stood next to her, brooding. From further along the bar, Evans cleared his throat, trying to catch Margaret's attention. She ignored him.

'I suppose you checked whether that bottle was poisoned or not, sister dear?'

Ingrid looked startled, and gaped at her in horror.

'You don't mean…?'

Margaret looked at her in triumph.

'I knew you'd be over here sooner or later, and you're the only one that drinks that muck… that - what is it… Nut Brown Sherry? I came over last week and popped some rat poison into the bottle. Couldn't you taste it?'

Ingrid struggled off her bar stool, and started coughing.

'You didn't?' She dropped the glass on the bar and spilt what was left on the counter. 'I always knew you were mad, Margaret! You're a fiend! You've murdered me… your own sister!'

Margaret sniffed.

'Unfortunately not! I was going to, but Evans stopped me… didn't you Evans?'

The manager appeared behind the bar again, looking agitated.

'Now Miss Margaret, not in front of the customers if you don't mind.'

He nodded over to the corner where Graham Blood sat, apparently oblivious, his head deep in the paper. Margaret looked over and took him in for the first time.

'A stranger in our midst, Evans! You should have warned me!'

'I tried to, Miss Margaret, but it doesn't matter.' He dropped his voice. 'Miss Ingrid has engaged the young gentleman over there to do some handyman work over at the Ridge. He'll be over this afternoon.'

'Oh, will he?' She turned to her sister, who was recovering herself. 'I must say, Ingrid, you should have consulted me first. You know very well...'

Ingrid thrust her face into her sister's line of vision.

'Don't say another word! I think you've said enough today, already.' She dropped her voice. 'I'm sick of living in a house that's gradually falling apart through lack of maintenance. At the very least we can get a few things fixed and working again.'

Margaret stared at her and relaxed somewhat.

'I thought you might be thinking of… Jane!'

'Not at all. This is purely practical,' Ingrid replied.

Margaret took this in, composed herself then turned and stalked majestically out through the door into the street.

Ingrid looked uncertain for a moment. Then she turned and stared again at Graham Blood, tossed her head at Evans, and followed her sister out.

Evans stood and polished Ingrid's discarded glass behind the bar, and shook his head. He was middle-aged and rather portly, with a few strands of hair that he had combed meticulously across his head from right to left. He looked harassed behind his sad little moustache.

Graham looked up, shortly, and gave the manager a quizzical look.

'Barmy?' he enquired, with a slow grin.

'Dangerous,' muttered the manager, 'and that's worse than barmy! They'll kill one another one of these days. If I were you, sir, I wouldn't go over there! There's a lot of funny things gone on in that house, you mark my words. None of the locals ever go there.'

Graham tried to make his mind up if the landlord was being serious.

'Well, who does go there? Surely…'

'No! Nobody! I don't think they've had a visitor in twenty years. They're a queer pair… not surprising considering the stock they come from. The old man, Theodore; the one Miss Ingrid was talking about, was a bit of a hermit. He was incredibly rich, but when he died – in South Africa, actually, or so the story goes – he left only a small portion of what people thought he had. The bulk of his fortune just disappeared. But he was a right old miser by all accounts, so he probably took it with him.'

'But that must have been over a hundred years ago?'

'1883! He was over in Kimberley on business, and the next thing, he died – from some strange malady. So they shipped him back in a barrel of port. Good for preserving the skin, so they say. Not so good for the port, though I do believe that his son, Gunther, refused to throw it out, and kept drinking the stuff for years afterwards. Germans, you know,' Evans said, giving Graham a knowing look. 'Eat their own grandmother's for tuppence.'

Graham grinned, showing a fine set of teeth.

'I meant to ask you, but it was late when I got in last night… Don't you have TV in your rooms? A bit strange in this day and age.'

Evans leant on his elbows and shook his head.

'There's no television in Heaven's Ridge! The ladies don't approve of new-fangled things, and this pub belongs to them. I don't even have the radio on when they're in earshot. It would be more than my license is worth.'

'Stranger and stranger,' said Graham, raising an eyebrow. 'Television – new-fangled? It's been around for fifty years.'

'True! But you've got to realize that these two dears not only live in the past, they live back in the days of great-great-grandad Theodore. He was such a larger than life figure that the family never got over him. The very fact that his son, Gunther, spent his whole life looking for a 'hidden hoard', just emphasized the fact. The more you get to know about the family, the more you realize there's something basically wrong with the lot of them... not that I said that, you understand! I just want a quiet life.'

'Don't worry, I won't repeat anything you say. But I must admit, I *am* intrigued. You talk about this family as if they were the only ones in Heaven's Ridge. How many are there?'

Evans looked pensive, and polished another glass.

'There are the two sisters, Margaret and Ingrid. They live in the main house and fight like cat and dog. There was another sister, Helen, but she got herself into trouble with a travelling salesman, and he left her in the lurch. She died in childbirth, back in the seventies. The baby lived though. She's in her twenties now, still living with her aunts over there. Interesting girl.'

'Oh, yes... what's her name?'

'Jane... Jane Wiltshire! At least, that's the name they gave her. The fellow's name was actually Will Shire. He took off into the great beyond, and never reappeared. So they called her Wiltshire.'

'Interesting variation,' said Graham.

'Yeah! A pity they wouldn't let her go!'

Graham looked puzzled. Evans noted his confusion.

'You'll find out, if you go over there. You'll probably find out a lot of things.'

'Yes, well... you were saying?'

'Oh yeah! There's also a cousin, Emerald. Another spinster! She lives in the little cottage over the other side of the road. She's from the collateral branch of the family, descended from

16

Theodore's second son, Frederick. She doesn't get on with the other two, and they don't get on with her. I think there's a bit of jealousy there that the sisters ended up with the big house, and she ended up with the cottage.'

'Who else,' said Graham.

'That's about it. The mechanic lives in one cottage with his wife, and the lady who runs the deli lives in the other. The closest town is forty kilometers away. We just see the odd prospector here and there. They use the pub while they're in the area, but we don't exactly make a fortune here. It's a backwater's backwater, if you know what I mean.'

Graham nodded in agreement.

'I think I gathered that. So why do *you* stay here?'

'It's peaceful,' said Evans. 'Well, that's what we tell the tourists, anyway. The other reason is gold.'

'There's gold in them thar hills – is that it?' said Graham, grinning.

'You can laugh, but old Theodore knew his onions. That house is built on what was once a solid ridge of gold. It's worked out now, of course, but gold doesn't appear in isolation. We've been hoping for another big strike in the area for over a hundred years. That's why I go out every weekend scouring the area with a metal detector.'

'You really think it's there. Another ridge of gold?'

'I'm not ready to give up yet. I just think we haven't gone deep enough. But there's plenty of time.'

Graham nodded, and continued to nod as if in answer to some private thought of his own.

'I think I will go over there,' he said. 'I might as well. You never know, it might be interesting.' He gave a cursory wave with his rolled newspaper, and Evans nodded as his guest headed out the door.

II

When Margaret swept out through the door of the hotel, she knew she wouldn't get very far before Ingrid came billowing after her. She was right. She let Ingrid catch up, then turned on her.

'You had no right to do that. You put me in an invidious position.'

'No, you put yourself in an invidious position, you and your mouth. Going on about poisoning the sherry! What will people think of us?'

'Well you ask for it most of the time. You make me want to kill you, sometimes.'

'That's lovely that is. Just slow down a bit, I'm trying to talk to you.'

Margaret maintained her pace, but looked back over her shoulder.

'You didn't want to talk to me this morning, you stomped out. Why would you want to talk to me now?'

'What's this rubbish about Jane? I never said anything about Jane!'

'Nobody said you did. It was just a thought. What's this idea of inviting young men back to the house? You know how I feel about strangers around the place. You've never done it before, why now?'

'Don't you think it's time we had a few repairs done, before the house falls down? I, for one, am sick of living in a house where nothing works anymore.'

Margaret turned, and tugged at Ingrid's sleeve.

'Oh no! That's not it at all. You've got your eye on him, Ingrid. Even now, after all these years, you still can't keep your hands to yourself.'

Ingrid stopped in the middle of the road, drew herself haughtily to her full height and looked up at Margaret.

'How dare you! Accusing me of *that*, at my age! I'll have you know that I haven't touched a man for over twenty years.'

'Only because of mother,' Margaret shot back. 'Mother used to have to lock you up! I remember. She called you a hussy and a tart!'

'And she didn't call you a little slut from time to time?'

'Mother was a fool,' Margaret snapped, pushing Ingrid away and continuing her charge up the road. 'If anyone was a tart and a little slut, Ingrid, it was you. I can remember that Johnny Morrison, back in the sixties, that drummer. You fell for him hook, line and sinker. We all know what happened that day, behind the old shed…'

'Nothing happened,' Ingrid wailed, 'Nothing! If only it had! I would be away from here, free of you! I would have left and never come back.'

Margaret turned and looked at Ingrid in contempt.

'He would have dumped you! The moment he found out what you were really like, he would have dumped you for good.'

'That's not true.' Ingrid half ran forward and grabbed Margaret by the arm again. 'You take that back, you bitch, you just take that back.'

'Get your hands off me,' said Margaret, madly flailing her arms to beat Ingrid off. 'It's true. He told me so – at the time. He wasn't really interested in you anyway. He was only using you to get to me. He said I had more class – that's what he said.'

Ingrid stopped, her mouth agape. Then she twisted her mouth into a grimace.

'I should kill you for that, Margaret! You spoil everything, you always have. You take a thing of beauty and you crush it and destroy it and spoil it forever. I'll wait until you're asleep one night and then I'll come creeping in with a hammer and I'll smash your brains all over the pillow. I'll do what I should have done years ago. I'll cut your throat with a cleaver and chop you up into little pieces!'

Ingrid's voice was gradually rising to a scream, and Margaret suddenly took off up the driveway, running for all she was worth. Ingrid followed her for a few paces, then stopped and yelled after her.

'You can't run away for ever, Margaret! You've got to sleep some time! I'm going to cut your legs off so you can't run, you... you... *bitch!*'

Margaret let out a yelp of terror, and glanced over her shoulder as she ran. She arrived at the front door of the house and rushed through it a good minute and a half before Ingrid finished stomping along the driveway, bending to the ground occasionally and picking up stones to throw at the house. Then Ingrid let herself in and slammed the door behind her.

Chapter Two

As Graham walked along the road towards Heaven's Ridge, he took in the view over the edge of what had once been a cliff, at a stage in the world's history when gulf waters had lapped at its base, some thousands of years before. The waters had since receded hundreds of miles, leaving behind a wide, sandy beach and a dry seabed. Between the road and the scrubby saltbush below the ridge was a hundred-foot drop, however, and the house enjoyed the most elevated view in the vicinity. Hidden behind an overgrown hedge and straggly eucalypts, it stood like a black shadow on top of the ridge, brooding and gloomy in its aspect.

The overhang of the roof had been designed to prevent the sun entering the windows at any time of the day during the summer months of the year. The roof was steeply pitched, and made of corrugated iron. From it, several tall chimneys made from natural stone climbed high into the air, and gleamed white in the sun. As Graham approached along the neglected driveway, he noted that only a few yards separated the house from the edge of the cliff. From where he stood it was starkly beautiful, but also somewhat overwhelming and sinister. There was no sign of life, and he hesitated before approaching the front door and giving the old brass knocker a resounding rap against the base plate.

As he waited for a response, he could hear various fumblings in the house, as if deep in its depths. Then he heard an inner door open, and the unmistakable sound of footsteps along a slated hallway. When the door opened, he was surprised to see the sister, Margaret, rather than the one who had suggested he call over.

'I understand you were invited to come over here in the capacity of an odd-job man,' Margaret said, looking along her nose at him. She seemed to be sizing him up, and pursed her lips as if coming to a decision regarding his visit.

'You do understand that my sister did not consult me in this beforehand. If she had, I would have, no doubt, expressly forbidden such a thing. We don't take kindly to strangers, Mister....?'

'Blood! Graham Blood,' said Graham, smiling and showing off his fine, white teeth. 'If this isn't a good time for you, I'd be quite happy to defer it until another time,' he said. He shrugged, as if her decision, one way or another, didn't make a great deal of difference. He was, after all, responding to a request for help. Apart from making a few dollars, which he patently was not in need of, the only draw for him was one of curiosity. He had time to burn, and precious little to do with it.

Margaret stood back, and opened the door a little wider.

'Oh, well, I don't suppose it can hurt. We do need a few things repaired around here, and your efforts will be well rewarded.' She flashed a sudden, overwhelming smile that transformed her face. But it was gone as quickly as it came.

'Follow me, please.'

Graham entered, and waited for her to lead him along the corridor. He'd been in these old places before, and didn't think that anything about the house would surprise him. He was wrong there. Instead of the usual four-square design of three bedrooms and a lounge with a central passage through to kitchen and bathroom etc., a second passage ran off to the left between the first and second doors on the left. They walked on past this, continued through the door at the end and found themselves in a sort of foyer area with passages running off in three directions.

Graham gave off a gasp of surprise, and Margaret was quick to respond.

'I see you are surprised at the extent of the house, Mr. Blood. It's very deceptive, isn't it - *'cunningly constructed',* as my sister would put it. The old kitchen runs directly off this foyer, then the three passages lead to different areas of the house. The passage to the right is out of bounds to you at all times. I mention this now so there will be no cause for regret later on. This first passage to the left takes us to the laundry, sewing room, and guest room. Then there is a door out into the garden where there are various outbuildings and some shedding. The second corridor takes us to an old, informal dining room, a second, formal dining room which is always kept locked, and an old 'punishment' room.'

Graham left out a whistle of surprise. Margaret stopped and looked at him intently.

'Oh, that's just what we call it. Succeeding generations of parents have used it to lock naughty children in there as punishment. Both Ingrid and I were locked in there as children at various times, when we wouldn't do as we were told. It's unused today. We're going to the kitchen, where my sister is going to give you instructions on whatever needs doing around the house.'

The kitchen turned out to be an old country kitchen with a massive wood-fired range, big enough to cater for parties. The walls were lined with cupboards, of which the doors of some were hanging from their hinges. There was an air of neglect about the place, and not a modern appliance to be seen. Margaret sat down at a central wooden table, where she had been shelling peas. At that moment Ingrid appeared at the door and smiled at him.

'Ah, Mister Blood. You've taken me up on my offer! I'm so pleased.' She looked around ruefully at the cupboards. 'As you can see, we spinsters are not so handy with screwdrivers and tools. Things tend to fall apart, and once they do are rarely fixed. Start anywhere you like, but perhaps the cupboard doors would be a good place to begin. You'll find a complete set of tools in the bottom cupboard over there, and various screws and nails in tins. Our late father kept them there.'

Margaret glared at her from where she sat, and Ingrid turned and left the room without another word.

Graham found an assortment of ancient tools in the prescribed cupboard, and couldn't help a gentle smile as he calculated their age. Some of these tools must have been a hundred years old, others over fifty. He looked up.

'These will do for now, but I have a few tools of my own in the boot of my car. I'll bring them over tomorrow. It might make things a little easier.'

'If you wish,' Margaret replied. She seemed a cold sort of fish.

While fixing the cupboard hinges he studiously avoided looking at Margaret, but thought he could feel her eyes boring into the back of his neck. When he did look around, she was still shelling peas, her eyes cast down to the table.

'I notice you don't have a refrigerator. How do you manage to keep things fresh out here? It must be terribly hot in summer.'

Margaret looked up, and laid her knife on the table.

'Neither my parents nor my grandparents believed in new fangle-dangles Mister Blood. We were brought up to do things in the old time-honoured ways, and we still stick to these principles. There's enough wickedness in the world without importing modern evils into Heaven's Ridge.'

Graham hardly knew what to say. How anyone could equate a refrigerator with evil was beyond him, but it was an enlightening moment in his struggle to understand these two women.

'Doesn't the meat go off… and the milk,' he ventured.

'We keep all those sorts of consumables down in the cellar, Mister Blood. You get there through that door at the end of the kitchen. There's a set of steps that leads down, and the temperature down there is never higher than three or four degrees above freezing. It's very cold, too cold sometimes. In the middle of winter I have to put on a woolly to avoid catching a cold. We need some repairs to the meat safe that's down there, so you'll be seeing it for yourself shortly.'

They were both silent for a minute or so while he fixed the final cupboard door.

'The manager at the hotel tells me that you don't approve of television.'

Margaret sat bolt upright in her chair.

'The manager of the hotel had no right to be discussing us, or our affairs with a total stranger, Mister Blood. I shall have a word with him.'

Graham looked suitably chastened.

'I'm sorry. I didn't know you were so sensitive, or I wouldn't have said anything.'

'I'm not aware that I'm any more sensitive than most, Mister Blood, but there are the proprieties to be considered, and it's most improper to discuss other people's business with any Tom, Dick or Harry that comes along. No offence intended.'

'None taken, I'm sure,' said Graham, raising one eyebrow to himself as he kept his back to her. 'Though I must confess that those types of restraints don't seem to apply in the modern world. Everybody talks about everyone else where I come from, and no one seems to get upset about it.'

'Which is why we prefer to keep ourselves cut off from the modern world and all its blasphemies,' said Margaret, righteously. 'We have no truck with evil, Mister Blood. As my father used to say – "if you sup with the devil, be sure to sup with a long spoon." '

At that moment Ingrid came pacing back into the kitchen. She flashed a look at Margaret, then at Graham just tidying up after himself.

'I see you've finished the cupboard doors, Mister Blood. If you'd care to come with me I'll show you a shed that needs the door fixing. It blew off in a storm two years ago, and the weather's getting in.'

Margaret gave Ingrid a silent, angry look.

'I have plenty of jobs for Mister Blood to do in here, Ingrid.'

Ingrid waved her objection aside.

'This is more important. He can come and do this one for me, then you may have him back for your jobs later.'

Margaret opened her mouth as if to protest, but then had second thoughts and shut it again. She went back to her peas, scowling.

Ingrid ushered Graham out of the kitchen and led him along one of the passages. They went through a door at the end, and suddenly they were in a garden at the rear of the house. There was an extensive lawn, tall fences and the odd eucalypt. Some thirty yards down the back of the garden there was a cluster of three sheds, one of which was missing a door. They were very old sheds, made predominantly of timber and corrugated iron. The doors were wooden and hinged, the hinges having mostly rusted away.

'As you can see, Mister Blood, they're in very poor condition. We really should have had someone in to see about them long before this, but as Margaret has no doubt told you, we don't encourage strangers. We're too old and fixed in our ways to change now.'

'Do you have new hinges for them?'

'As a matter of fact, we do. My father bought new hinges before he died, with the intention of fixing all of them. But he didn't get around to it.'

She led him into the shed without the door, and pointed out a workbench along the far wall on which lay six faded packets containing new hinges.

'Just when did your father die… as a matter of interest,' said Graham, turning one of the packets over in his hand. It was dusty, and the printed backing had faded considerably.

'It was… let me see! Oh, back in 1980. He had a heart attack, and died at the dinner table. He was only fifty-four. It seems like only yesterday. It was a great shock to us all, as you can well imagine. My poor mother was at her wits end, worrying about how we should manage, just three females and a five-year-old child. But luckily we got over that feeling of dependence on having a man about the place, and when mother died four years later, we hardly noticed it.'

'A child, you said.' Graham looked at her studiously, as if willing her to continue.

'Yes, Jane! She's about here somewhere. No doubt you'll run into her sooner or later. My younger sister's daughter! Helen died in childbirth, and we were left to bring Jane up. It was difficult at times, but we managed.'

'So… if she was five in 1980, she must be about twenty-five now,' Graham said, cautiously.

'That's right… Or she will be, in October. She's a strange child, mind you. If she speaks to you at all, you may get the impression that she's a little bit weird. That's merely because she's led a very sheltered life here. We had to attend to her education ourselves after the age of eleven… since the accident. She couldn't travel after that. And children are so cruel. Anyone who has a disability, or who is deformed in any way, is always the butt of their jokes. We didn't think Jane could cope with it, so we brought her home and gave her lessons ourselves.'

'Didn't the authorities kick up about that?'

'Not too many authorities up this way, as you can imagine. And that's the way we like it. We're a very independent family, Mister Blood, and hate being told what to do. My grandfather hated bureaucrats, so did my father. I don't think we've put a tax return in for over fifty years. None of their business, anyway!'

'I wish that worked for me,' Graham grinned. Ingrid thought he had a most disarming smile.

She went quite weak at the knees at that moment, and turned away in confusion.

'Well, if you'll just fix this door, Mister Blood. Then, if you would, replace the hinges on all the other shed doors.'

She stood back, outside the shed, and twisted her fingers together, nervously. She seemed undecided whether to stay or go. Graham looked at her, standing in the sunlight, and suddenly realized that for her age, Ingrid was remarkably attractive. She had a bright red spot in each cheek, and though her hair was tied back in a bun, she had no grey hair. It was brown with red lights. When she smiled, her cheeks dimpled, and she had deep grey eyes, like pools. There was something very sad about those eyes.

'I do wish you'd call me Graham,' he said. 'I'm not used to all this formality. The only person that ever calls me Mister Blood is the bank manager, and that's usually when he's not very happy with me.'

Ingrid laughed, a tinkling laugh that sounded more like a young girl than a middle-aged woman. Then she put her hand over her mouth as if she had committed a *faux pas*, and turned side on, looking across the garden.

'I, err… I don't know if that would be quite proper, Mister….'

'Oh, proper be damned! You've been out of the world too long, Ingrid. You don't mind if I call you Ingrid, do you?'

Ingrid blushed, and shook her head in confusion.

'No… no, I don't mind. In fact… in fact I quite like it.'

'Good! Well, in that case, Ingrid, I insist on you calling me Graham. Is that a deal?'

Ingrid nodded, her eyes cast down to the lawn. She could feel the flush on her cheeks, and that embarrassed her. She was forty-two years old, and still blushed when a man called her by her first name. How ridiculous! At the same time she was aware of stirrings in various parts of her body that had been closed down for over twenty years, and this brought a confusion to her mind that interfered with her thought processes, and made her feel idiotic.

'Very well… Graham! I suppose you'll be around for a few days, so we'll get used to each other shortly.'

Graham pulled the old door into position, and began to attach the new hinges.

'I must admit, you interest me very much, both you and your sister. I mean, it must have been very difficult for you here, away from the world so to speak. You've pretty well lived your lives in isolation. It's obvious that neither of you have ever been married, probably never had the opportunity. But didn't you ever feel the urge... to get away from here? To go and see what the world was about?'

Ingrid suddenly stiffened, and stood stock still. It was as if he had just slapped her in the face.

'Really! Really, Mister Blood! Oh dear!'

She turned on her heel and hurried off across the lawn. Graham stared after her, wondering what it was he could have said to upset her so much. Although he could only see her from behind, it was obvious that she was weeping as she entered the house. The door slammed behind her.

'Me and my bloody big mouth,' he muttered. Then he threw the hinges down onto the lawn and stamped his foot. 'How the hell do you deal with these people,' he mouthed to himself.

He began to pace up and down the lawn, thinking furiously. Shortly, the back door opened and Margaret swept down the garden towards him, looking haughty and indignant.

'What on earth did you say to my sister to upset her so,' she demanded.

Graham placed his palms upwards, and shook his head.

'I was just making conversation,' he said. 'I had no intention of upsetting her, no intention at all. I merely asked if she had ever felt the need to leave this place and go and see what the world was about.'

Margaret nodded grimly, but said nothing.

'Maybe it was because I said that, obviously, the two of you had never been married... I don't know. Is that a touchy subject?'

'Anything of a personal nature is a touchy subject, Mister Blood. I don't know where you were brought up, and I really don't want to know, but to engage a maiden lady in conversation and ask personal questions like that is about as inappropriate as you can get. Please keep your observations to the business in hand in future, and you will avoid this sort of upset.'

Graham looked distraught.

'Look, I'm sorry. I didn't mean anything by it. Where I come from people just talk. No one takes offence, or takes straightforwardness as a personal insult. I just put my thoughts into words, that's all. Obviously I'm going to be curious. That's human nature! It's just natural.'

'The lord said – *I am against you, natural man,*' Margaret replied, her eyelids half closed, her face raised to the heavens. 'In future, please use more discretion.'

Graham nodded, swallowing hard.

'I will, I will! Please apologize to Ingrid for me. I had no intention...'

'Ingrid! Since when did you start calling her Ingrid?'

'Well, just now... a while ago. I asked her if it would be all right, and she said yes. I mean – I'm not comfortable with all this formality. I told her to call me Graham.'

'I sincerely hope she refused!'

'No – as a matter of fact she didn't. But then she got all upset.'

'I will be having a word with her! In future, *Miss* Ingrid if you don't mind, and *Miss* Margaret for myself. It states who we are, and also places a respectable distance between us, if you know what I mean.'

'I can assure you, I meant no disrespect,' said Graham.

'I'm sure you didn't,' Margaret said, softening her tone. 'But you must realize that the old ways are the best ways. They create no misunderstandings.'

She turned on her heel and strode off back to the house, her head held high. Graham stared after her in bemusement, and seriously considered whether to cut and run. After a few minutes he calmed down, and reflected that even if he wanted to quit, he would have to pass back through the house to get out, and he had no wish to run that gauntlet just yet. He persevered with the shed doors until the sun went down, then went warily back into the house and along the hallway. There was no sign of Ingrid.

Just as he opened the front door and tried to slip through, Margaret appeared from a side passage behind him and said, 'tomorrow morning… at nine o'clock?'

He just looked back and nodded, then closed the door quietly behind him and made his way pensively along the driveway. When he got to the hotel, instead of stopping in the bar he made his way directly to his room, flung himself down on his bed and stared, moodily, at the ceiling.

Chapter Three

Margaret went back inside and found Ingrid lying face down on her bed crying, as if there was no tomorrow. Something in her crusty demeanor softened, and she sat quietly on the edge of the bed, waiting for her sister to stop. Ingrid kept her face buried in the pillow, and made motions with her hands as if to tell her to go away, but Margaret was having none of it, and sat there stolidly, determined to be there when she recovered herself.

'Leave me alone can't you. Haven't you said enough today, already?'

Margaret cleared her throat and stared fixedly at the wall.

'I wouldn't have said what I did if you hadn't been so insulting, earlier. You really make my blood boil sometimes. For what it's worth, I didn't mean it. I never spoke to your Johnny Morrison, and he never spoke to me. He only had eyes for you, Ingrid. If it hadn't been for mother, I'm sure that he would have stuck by you and insisted you go off with him when he left for Adelaide. But he was too embarrassed by then. Mother was a real bitch!'

Ingrid stirred, and slowly lifted her head from the pillow. She looked slowly around at her sister, and Margaret noted her puffy eyes, red and swollen from crying. At that moment Ingrid looked very young, almost as young as she'd looked the night that she'd sat in the bar of the hotel, shyly holding hands with a young man that she'd only met the day before. Margaret remembered the way his long hair swept down over his shoulders, and how the lights gleamed back from the gold chain and bracelet that he wore, ostentatiously proclaiming his occupation as a rock star.

Ingrid had been a flower that night, a tiny, precious flower with flushed cheeks and an expression of awe on her teenage face, as he held her hand quietly beneath the table. She had sipped Vodka and orange through a straw for the first time in her life, and had felt her heart beating a rapid patter as her narrow life opened to the possibility of a future away from Heaven's Ridge.

Ingrid rolled over and sat up. She wiped her eyes with the back of her hand, and pushed Margaret's proffered handkerchief away.

'Well why did you say it, then? You're always saying horrible things to me, and it spoils everything, even the few decent memories I do have.'

'You can talk! How do you expect me to be when you're always threatening to chop off my legs? You really had me worried.'

Ingrid shook her head, exasperated.

'It's a game, a stupid game! You know it's a game! We've both done it... ever since that horrible day...'

'All right!' said Margaret, shielding her face with her hand. 'Don't! We said we'd never discuss it, and we never shall. It's best forgotten.'

Ingrid put her face up close to her sister's, and glared at her.

'How can you forget something like that? How? We're both going to hell, Margaret! One day we're going to wake up in a pool of fire, with flames licking around us and peeling all our skin from our bones. Forever, Margaret! We're going to burn forever!'

Margaret jumped to her feet and in an agony of denial shook uncontrollably on the spot.

'Don't! Stop torturing us, Ingrid. When we die, we'll just be dead, that's all. And if we're truly penitent, we'll be forgiven all our sins. It says in the Bible that when you die, it is as if you had never been. It doesn't say anything about pits of fire…'

'…Or devils, poking you with their tridents, Margaret. But those stories must have come from somewhere. Danté wasn't the only one that saw hell as a place of eternal fire and damnation.'

'Stop this, Ingrid. You're making our lives miserable with your doom and gloom. I don't want to talk about that any more. I came in to talk about what happened out there, in the garden. Why did he upset you so much?'

Ingrid slumped on the bed, and looked down at her hands. She was quiet for a moment, as if she didn't have the words to express what she'd felt.

'It's… hard! I suddenly felt so completely useless. When he said that *'obviously'* we'd never been married, I suddenly thought… is it so obvious then? Are we so different to everyone else because we've never had a man in our lives? I suddenly felt that I must be wearing a stamp on my forehead saying *'Virgin! Useless! Pathetic old tart! Empty and useless old shell!'* I suppose I thought of those peas you were shelling on the kitchen table. There you were, splitting open those ripe pods with your fingers and squeezing out all those little baby peas, as if from a womb. Then you threw the empty pod to one side, and went on with the next. Is that what we are... empty pods? No baby peas in us, Margaret, or if there were, they're long gone now. We're just those useless, empty shells that people throw away. It's as if we missed our prime purpose in life. We denied ourselves those gifts that God gave us, and here we are, a couple of middle-aged spinsters. Spinsters! Even the word smacks of impoverishment. What is a spinster? One of those old hags from the old days that eked out a living over a spinning wheel, with no one to love or protect them in their old age, just loneliness and a feeling of fruitlessness. That's what we are, Margaret, fruitless. *Our fruit has withered on the vine,* and we are left to the tender mercies of each other in the fading years of our lives. Never to have felt the body of a man lying next to us in bed. Never to...'

'That's quite enough, Ingrid. We are what we are, and nothing is now going to change that. We can thank our mother largely for the way we turned out. She brought us up, after all. She impressed her own ideas on our blank, empty souls. If you want to blame anyone, blame mother. I do! Do you know, Ingrid, I sometimes sit here at night in this old house, and I imagine her walking along the passageways in her bare feet, lost, and calling out for someone, anyone to come and lead her away. I think she was a lost soul herself, and she impressed that void, that emptiness on us. She didn't want us to succeed where she had failed, Ingrid. She couldn't bear the thought that we might go off into the world and find happiness, when she herself had been imprisoned in this house from the age of seventeen, which was when she married our father. She wanted to keep us here, Ingrid, to look after her and keep her company when father had gone. And that's why I think I hate her! I hate her, Ingrid, because she's gone, and we're still here!'

Margaret suddenly stopped, and Ingrid saw the tears pouring down her cheeks, and her lips quivering in some intense emotion.

'I had no idea… that you felt like that, Margaret. No idea! I thought you were the strong one.'

Margaret barked out a sardonic laugh, and blew her nose on her hanky.

'No, you have no idea, Ingrid. You're right there. Our mother was sick, sick and perverted. She had this air of virginal goodness about her that she carried around like a halo. Did you know that she made me bathe, as a child, in my drawers? True! She taught me that it was sinful to touch myself down there, and that if I did, I would break out in big weeping sores and die. She said it was naughty and bad, and that I must never look in the mirror at my naked body, or touch myself. As I grew up, she put it into my head that men were dirty animals, and that all they wanted to do was to touch you down there, and make you unclean. For a while there, during puberty, I became obsessed with myself, and when I began to bleed I thought I'd done some terrible thing to myself, and God was punishing me. I thought I was going to bleed to death! I was too ashamed to tell mother, and she only found out one day when I bled so badly that it ran down my leg and made a mess on the kitchen floor. Then she told me about towels, and that I was a woman now. After scaring me half to death during my childhood, she finally made out there was nothing wrong, and it was all quite natural. I felt sick to my stomach. Then when I met a prospector's son down in the sandhills, when I was thirteen, he put a hand on my leg and I screamed and screamed until he ran away. I never did let anyone touch me after that.'

Ingrid leaned over and put her arm around Margaret's shoulder.

'I'm sorry… so sorry,' she said, fighting back her own tears. 'I had no idea. She must have brought me up differently to you, because she never made me bathe like that, and she never told me that it was bad. She just never said anything.'

'That's because you were father's favourite. He used to carry you around with him like a big cuddly toy, so mother never got near you. I think she was jealous of you, do you know that? She took her guilt complex out on me, but she was jealous of you because you took up too much of father's attention. That's why she took Johnny Morrison away. It was like a revenge thing.'

Ingrid sat up straight, a quizzical look on her face.

'What do you mean by that? What do you mean… *took him away?*'

Margaret sat up, and shook her head in confusion.

'I didn't mean that, it was just an expression.'

'No… come on, Margaret. You've started now, you just tell me what you meant by that.'

'I didn't mean anything, really! Look, it's no good getting you all upset again. I think we've both had enough emotion for one day. I'll tell Mister Blood to come back tomorrow and he can carry on as if nothing's happened. We'll just keep it nice and formal, that way no one gets upset.'

'No, Margaret. You were talking about the one event in my life that meant anything to me, and you obviously know something that I don't. I think that after all these years I at least deserve to share in the family secrets, don't you? If you know more than I do, then spit it out. Don't worry, I can take it!'

Margaret looked gingerly at Ingrid, then sighed, and pulled a face.

'I shouldn't have said anything. It was a long time ago, and after all, mother's dead! Nothing matters anymore. Why can't you just let it rest?'

'Because it concerns me,' said Ingrid, glaring. 'It's about a moment in my life that I cherish in my memory... the *only* moment, in fact, that I cherish. He was so handsome,' she sighed, shaking her head in reflection. 'Do you remember? All the fellows had long hair in those days. They were beautiful. Don't you think they were beautiful?'

Margaret didn't reply. She was dreading the remainder of this conversation.

'I remember sitting in the hotel, holding his hand. He was only staying there for a couple of days, because the group's van had broken down.

Some of the others had hitch-hiked on to Adelaide, but he'd chosen to stay with the van. They'd played some concerts – did they call them concerts then, or was it 'gigs'? Anyway, they'd played in Perth, and were on their way to record some new songs in Adelaide. He was full of it. He said they were the best songs they'd ever written. I never did get to hear them!'

She spoke the last plaintively, as if that was a source of great regret. She was silent for a moment, then went on.

'I remember going for a walk with him, and then later we went back to the house and I introduced him to mother. She was in one of her funny moods, drifting about the place like a ghost in one of those filmy things she used to wear when she got depressed. I don't know if she even noticed him, really. She let him kiss her hand then drifted off into the kitchen for some reason or other. We went out in the garden, and strolled around. Then I remember standing with my back to the side of the shed, and him towering over me. That was when he kissed me.'

Ingrid shuddered as if she could still feel that kiss, that one long, lingering kiss on an autumn night in the back garden, just as it was getting dark.

'Then he put his arms around me and held me... he just held me,' she sighed. 'He felt so strong. And he had this beautiful, musky smell about him. It was so... masculine!' she finally decided was the word she required. 'So masculine! I felt so warm and protected in his arms. I'd never realized it could feel like that. Then we went back into the house, and mother was really sweet for a change. She said there was no point in him going back to the hotel, that he could stay in the guest room that night, and I was so happy. Father was away at the time, I remember. Away on one of his trips! Mother was usually funny when he went away, but this time she was really very sweet. She cooked dinner for us all, but you'd remember that. You were there, at the table. I remember we laughed a lot, even mother, and I really don't remember her as being the sort of person who laughed very much at all. So she must have been glad of the company. Do you remember, Margaret?'

'Like yesterday,' said Margaret, dully. Ingrid waited for her to continue, but Margaret kept silent.

'All right. Now tell me what you were going to say before. What was this about mother *'taking him away?'* Just what did you mean by that?'

'I don't think you really want to know, Ingrid. You'll just take it out on me, and it was nothing to do with me. I was just an innocent bystander.'

'Just tell me,' Ingrid snapped, coming to the end of her patience. Margaret shook her head again, but reluctantly began to speak.

'Well, you remember the day pretty well, but do you remember what happened the next day?'

'Yes. He took off without even saying goodbye. I was really hurt. I thought that those moments had meant something to him, but obviously they hadn't. I was just a stupid little star-struck girl, totally naïve in the ways of the world.'

'I only wish you were right… about him, I mean. Oh, you were naïve all right, but not about him. You were naïve about mother, and the lengths she would go to.'

'I'm listening,' said Ingrid, after a long, uncomfortable pause.

'Well, the fact is, she didn't want you to go. She knew it was a dangerous situation, and who knows, she was probably right. Those rock stars could have any girl they wanted. You would have been okay for a month or two, until he tired of you, or found another little star-struck angel that appealed to him more. Then he would probably

51

have fobbed you off with some excuse. Or maybe you would have married him, and spent the next few years being lied to and miserable, while he played around. They're not the most stable of people.'

'Go on,' said Ingrid, cautiously.

'I suppose she could have been thinking about your welfare... or maybe she was more concerned with not having you around to look after her in her old age. Who knows? But you need to remember that mother was not an old woman at the time. She was relatively young, and she was a good looking woman, you've got to give her that.'

'What's that got to do with it? He just took off! When I got up the next morning, he'd already gone. The publican, old Mister Hayes, said he'd hitch-hiked to Adelaide that morning, and then a couple of days later someone else came back to pick up the van. I never saw or heard from him again. I remember I was heart-broken.'

'But not horrified, not shocked like I was. Do you remember where I was that morning – and remember, I was about twenty-three then! Twenty-three years old!'

Ingrid thought back, back through the years to that desperate morning when she was seventeen, and young, fresh, and naïve.

'Yes,' she said slowly. 'Yes, I remember. You were locked in the punishment room. I never did find out what for. I thought it was rather strange at the time, but nobody was saying anything.'

'I was locked in the punishment room so I'd keep my mouth shut. You see I'd caught them… together.'

Ingrid looked incredulous. She pulled away from her sister and looked at her as if she was mad.

'What do you mean, together? You don't mean…'

Margaret nodded her head, miserably. It was finally out, the dreaded secret that she'd carried around with her for twenty-five years.

'I couldn't sleep! I hate to admit it, but I was very jealous of you, and I thought that it was unfair that you should have a young man when I was the older one, and I had no one. So at one o'clock in the morning I crept out of bed and made my way along the passage to the guest room. I was in bare feet, and moved very quietly. I remember looking up and down the passage with my hand on the door handle, then I opened the door.'

Ingrid picked up the pillow, hugged it to her chest and bit on the corner.

'What happened? What happened then?'

'I opened the door, and there was a bedside lamp on. There was mother, kneeling astride your young man and bouncing up and down, shaking her head around and panting like a dog. I didn't know... I mean, I really *didn't* understand what they were doing! I had no idea that women got on top and that men lay flat on their backs. I was so innocent.'

Margaret put her hands to her ears as if to drown out the sounds of her mother making love, all those years ago. Ingrid let out a despairing moan, and rolled over on the bed, hugging the pillow to her breast.

'She went crazy! I just stood there, petrified. I couldn't move. I suppose I was in shock, but for the life of me I felt as if I was glued to the floor. Every instinct told me to run, but I couldn't. I just stood there, staring and staring, as she climbed off him and came for me with her nails. She slapped my face and clawed all my neck, then dragged me off and locked me in the punishment room. Before she went she said I was to forget everything I'd seen… it hadn't happened. The next day, before she let me out, she came in with a cane and made me bend over that old cage in there, and pull my skirt up. Then she caned me, four times on my bottom. And she called me a slut, a filthy swine of a slut. She said I had a dirty mind or I wouldn't have just stood there, looking. Then she said that if I said anything to my father, he would send me to a girl's home, and I would be locked up and beaten by nuns every day. By the time she finished with me I was in abject terror. It was as if I had been the one committing the sin, not her. Just by going to his room in the middle of the night, she said, I was a strumpet, a hussy, and that God would make me pay for my sinful mind. When I got out, your young man had gone, and she put the cane in the kitchen, on the floor, called me in and swore me to silence. She made me bend over and put my hands on the cane, and swear that if I said anything to you, she would cane me every day for a year. And I did! Like a silly young fool I did. I got down on my hands and knees and swore… *'if I say anything about this to Ingrid, I want you to cane me every day for a year.'* God… I hated that woman after that! I hated her, Ingrid. I really hated her!'

Ingrid peered over the top of her pillow, her eyes red and puffy, and nodded slowly as her sister sat on the bed and cried.

Chapter Four

The following morning, Graham woke up at six o'clock. This was unusual for him. He usually slept in until eight when working, or nine thirty on holidays. But the night before he had lain on his bed, pondering the strange circumstances of the day, and had fallen asleep without benefit of an evening meal. He woke up at ten and crawled into bed, strangely tired. He'd fallen asleep again the moment his head hit the pillow, and was awakened in the morning by the sound of a bird singing outside his window.

There was no sign of movement in the hotel, so he showered, dressed, and slipped out the back way, then finding the day to be sunny and bright thought he'd go for an early morning walk. He set off along the narrow main street in the opposite direction to 'Heaven's Ridge', thinking to work his way down and around to the beach that was so visible from the top of the cliff. To do this he had to walk downhill for half a mile, then take a track off to the right that led through saltbush and a scrubby, parched hillside. Finally he arrived at the bottom and struck out over the sandhills towards the ancient beach.

Halfway across he looked back and up at the towering cliff that had once, aeons ago, whispered to the sounds of an incoming tide. It now stood stark against the sky, deserted by the waters that had beaten against its rocky foundations and turned seashells into sand, many many thousands of years ago. It looked strangely out of place in that country, like a monolith of an ancient civilization that had moved on, and left it stranded in a moment of time when gods had roamed the surface of the earth. At its peak was the shadow of the house, built incongruously at the edge of nowhere.

Another ten minutes found him on the beach, surveying its long sweep, the drop away to a prehistoric seabed, and the rise again to a matching beach on the other side, some two miles away. This must have stood at or near the top of a gulf, as the distance between the opposing beaches narrowed as he looked south. Northwards they widened, then other cliffs and escarpments arose out of the sand and hid its course from view. Strange to think that once upon a time man may have traversed waters along this gulf in primitive boats made of hollowed out trees, or bark, cunningly sewn and patched with mud and clay. He wandered along the beach, kicking at the sand and finding plenty of evidence of an ancient seabed in the shape of shells, buried in the sand. He picked the odd one up here and there that caught his eye, and slipped them into his pockets. To think that they may have lain here for thousands of years, undisturbed, long after the organisms that inhabited them had wandered off the pages of history.

Graham was in a philosophical mood that morning. He was not used to being so utterly alone, and it produced in him a profound sense of himself as a being apart. The noises and interactions of normal life usually stifled any feelings of self as a unique entity attached to and within the universe, and as a result the spiritual side of his nature was rarely challenged. But the moment that the only dialogue possible was one that occurred deep inside him, between he and himself, the feeling of awe and strangeness grew by degrees until he felt the very spirit start to move in the inanimate things around him. He saw it move in the very rocks of the countryside, watched it soar in the ambient movement of an invisible breeze that filled the flaring feathers of the birds of the air. It raised them first to the blue heavens, then slipped through their wings to glide them along a path as caring and secure as the uplifting hand of God.

He stopped and looked up at the sky, and scratched his head. Where on earth was all this coming from? Graham Blood was not known for his philosophical musings, nor for any great profundity of thought. He didn't claim for himself any elevated intellectual airs; he was just a good bloke! An ordinary Joe, one who would rather repay a good turn than do someone a bad one. There must be something in the air out here to make him muse on such philosophical topics.

Then he thought of Ingrid. What a mystery she was! What a tangle of emotions and conbobulated self-regulation she must carry around as her life's baggage... *Conbobulated?* Yes, why not? If you came across something as alien as a set of rules that made no sense, but that affected another human being in such a devastating manner, then it was all right to make up a word to describe those rules, even if you were the only one it made sense to. Conbobulated! Totally bloody conbobulating! And that sister, Margaret. What a horror! No doubt, she knew all about conbobulation! She probably invented it.

Graham looked back at the clifftop, and peered into the shadow that followed the fences around on the cliff side of the house. Surely there was something moving there. He shaded his eyes and tried to focus. There was a break in the fence that looked like a gateway, right on the edge of the cliff. In the opening stood the figure of a woman.

She was slim and tall, and her long white dress billowed about her as she stood. It wasn't Ingrid. She was too tall for Ingrid. And it wasn't Margaret, unless she had suddenly taken off thirty years and turned into a siren. Graham nodded slowly to himself. It must be Jane... Jane Wiltshire. Strange that he hadn't seen her the day before. She must have been around but had chosen, for reasons of her own, not to show herself. Yet here she was, standing at the top of the cliff and looking down at him with apparently overwhelming interest.

He looked around to see if there was anything or anyone else on the beach that could have caught her eye, but he could see nothing. Nothing that she hadn't seen a million times before, at any rate. No, she was definitely looking at him, and he felt a crawling sensation at the base of his spine as the hairs rose in his consternation. What was it about that girl... woman! Of course, she was a woman, twenty-five years old, so Ingrid had said. What had Evans said at the pub? – *a pity they wouldn't let her go!'*

He'd made her sound like some sort of prisoner of the estate. But she couldn't be! There she was, out in the garden on her own, peering down at him through the gate. If she'd really wanted to leave, no doubt she could just walk away. She was a grown woman after all, not a child any longer.

As he watched, a figure came up behind her and he saw a hand clamp firmly down on her shoulder and spin her around. They stood face to face for a minute while words were apparently exchanged, then the tall figure stumbled back inside the gate, and her place was taken by the straight, unyielding form of the elder sister, Margaret. He continued to stare, and even though the distance was too great to make out any features, it seemed that Margaret's eyes swept across to where he stood, then without acknowledgement of any kind she stepped away and pulled the gate shut behind her.

Graham looked down and continued his pacing along the beach. Maybe that was why Ingrid had said, on his first entry to the house, that the right hand passage from the foyer was out of bounds to him at all times. Maybe that was where they kept Jane! Perhaps they'd kept her locked in her room all day while he was there. It was possible. For a couple of old maids like them, with their funny ideas about men, maybe they thought that a contact with him would contaminate the poor woman. He grinned to himself at the thought.

Up to that point he had been having definite reservations about spending another day with the sisters. He realized that the events of the afternoon's contretemps with Ingrid had depressed him no end, and he had thought of crying off for the day. But after catching that tantalizing glimpse of Jane Wiltshire, it was as if he had regained a sudden zest for the chase. Who could tell what was going to happen? Knowing now that she was definitely on the premises so to speak, he thought that it might not be such a bad thing to try to meet her, even if it embarrassed the two older women in some way. After all, what could they do except get upset all over again about some petty rule of behaviour that he was not privy to. He could just plead ignorance again, and things could go on as before. He turned back to the sandhills, looked up once again at Heaven's Ridge, then put his head down and plodded back the way he had come.

II

Emerald Schuman arose at five-thirty every morning without fail. She was then in the habit of showering, dressing and making a light breakfast of two pieces of toast, spread with thick butter, and one piece of toast with marmalade. To drink she always made a pot of tea in the old fashioned way. First warm the pot, then two heaped teaspoons of Ceylonese tea – she still called it Ceylonese, she didn't care that the natives had changed its time-honoured name – then add boiling water and let it brew for ten minutes. The first cup was always the best, and she savored that cup. After a second cup she would venture out into her tiny front garden and do a little weeding, and talk to her plants and flowers.

By this time it was between six thirty and six forty-five, and for three hundred and sixty four days of the year there would be nothing happening in the main street of Heaven's Ridge. That was the way she liked it. At fifty-six years of age, and a confirmed spinster like her cousins, she just wanted to be left alone to live out the rest of her days undisturbed.

On this, the three hundred and sixty fifth day of the year, a young man issued from the rear of the hotel across the road into the main street, looked both ways up and down the road, then set off in the opposite direction to Heaven's Ridge. He was on foot, so he was obviously going to the beach. There was nothing else in that direction except endless miles of road.

Emerald was crouching down over her tiny petunia patch when she saw him, and she peered curiously over the wall at him as he set off. There was something familiar about him, something very familiar. She creased her brow in an attempt to remember, but it just wouldn't come.

The day before, when he had wandered off up the road to her cousin's house, she had been in bed feeling rather poorly. So this was the first time she had actually seen him. But she had heard from old Evans at the pub, where she collected her weekly paper, that there was a young man in the hamlet, and that he had been engaged by her cousin Ingrid to effect some repairs up at the old house. This had made her intensely curious, as she was well aware how anti-social the two sisters had always been, even with their own flesh and blood.

Emerald had not always lived at Heaven's Ridge. She was the only living descendant of Theodore's second son, Frederick, who had gone off as a young man to work in the monster Burra copper mine, and later to Moonta, the richest copper mine in the world. That was where he had married Alice Stanley, who had borne his only son Lawrence, before he was murdered by his wife in 1900, poisoned with copper sulphate crystals. Alice hanged herself three days later, without leaving a note. Their three year old son was brought up by friends of the family.

Lawrence, Emerald's grandfather, also worked the Moonta Mine until the mine closed in 1923. It was that year that his second son Hayden was born. Hayden was Emerald's father. Hayden's older brother, Gordon, had been born in 1920, but died in 1925 under the wheels of the Moonta train. The closure of the mine, the birth of his second son and the loss of his first knocked the wind out of Lawrence's sails, and he opted to stay on in Moonta long after the majority of the miners had left for Broken Hill. He obtained employment in a menswear shop in George Street, and Hayden grew up in the town.

By the time Hayden came back from the second world war after serving in France, his father and mother had moved back to this little cottage in Heaven's Ridge, which had been left to them by Lawrence's uncle, Gunther. Hayden remained in Moonta, married a Wallaroo girl named Erika Huntly, and Emerald was born in 1946.

Her father died in 1964, her mother in 1985, and the little cottage was left to her. Being more than aware of her peculiar family history, she was only too happy to give up paying rent, move up to Heaven's Ridge, and try to re-acquaint herself with her cousins. This was in 1985. But Margaret and Ingrid proved to be not so accommodating as she had expected. They were not impressed with her credentials or her bloodline, and had made it clear that they just wished to be left alone.

At first hurt by their swift rejection, Emerald had started digging into the family tree, and began to ask questions about the legal ownership of Heaven's Ridge. She was under the impression that old great-great-grandfather Theodore had left Heaven's Ridge to his descendants *en masse*, and indeed, more than one family of Schuman's had inhabited the place in times gone by. This had not seemed to be a problem to earlier generations, but by the time Margaret and Ingrid inherited they maintained that the ownership of the house was their birthright alone, and that the most any other member of the family could expect was one of the small cottages further down the road.

Lacking the money to engage legal counsel, Emerald had withdrawn from the fray, wounded but not yet defeated. She still coveted a small part of the ownership of the old house, and would not, in her mind, give it up. She made a point of annoying the two sisters whenever they ventured along the road, and made cutting remarks about various things that had happened in the immediate past. As a result both Margaret and Ingrid avoided her whenever possible, and made it a rule to refuse her entry to the house. Many a time Emerald had been kept standing on the doorstep, while imparting another interesting bit of information about what she had discovered about the family history.

This particular morning she stood up and watched Graham's back as he wandered off along the road so early in the morning. There was something about the way that he walked, something... what on earth was it? Try as she might, it wouldn't come to her.

At 7.35 she got up off her knees, placed her trowel on the window ledge and went back inside. After washing her hands she carefully lifted down a large folder full of newspaper cuttings, photocopies of wills, deeds, birth, marriage and death certificates, and various data that she had managed to glean from the Mortlock Library of South Australia. Amongst all this was a large, hand-written family tree that she had painstakingly put together from the information she had gleaned. She ran her eye over this and suddenly jabbed her finger onto one name.

'That's it,' she said. 'That's it!'

She carefully returned the sheet to the folder, and put the folder back where she'd got it from. Then she went through to the bathroom, brushed her hair and tidied herself up. Within five minutes she was making her way along the road to Heaven's Ridge.

Margaret came to the door when it seemed like her summons was never going to be answered. She stared at her cousin with obvious dislike.

'Oh, it's you! I won't say I'm glad to see you. What do you want?'

'Now is that a way to treat a dear cousin? You really are quite rude, Margaret. I'm sure you don't talk to everyone like that.'

'I don't talk to anyone, Emerald. You should know that by now! As I've tried to explain to you many times, it's nothing personal. We just prefer our own company; that's all. It might have been different if you'd been brought up in Heaven's Ridge, as we were. But you can't create a bond that isn't there.'

'We share the same bloodlines, Margaret. That should count for something.'

'Perhaps it should, but in actual fact, it doesn't. You're just a stranger to us, Emerald, and we don't invite strangers into our house.'

'Now, that's not strictly correct, is it?' said Emerald, waving a finger meaningfully in the air. 'In fact you invited a total stranger into your house only yesterday, a young man I believe. Not someone you've ever seen before.'

Margaret leaned on the door-post as if exasperated, and bored.

'So you've found out about our odd-job man. How nice for you! Now, if you'll excuse me...'

'Not so fast, Margaret. Have you any idea who this young man is? I do!'

'What do you mean, you do? How can you know? Oh, I see, you've run into him before, in Moonta, perhaps? Well, that's not so very surprising. I believe he gets around a bit, may even come from Moonta for all I know. That's not important! What's important is what he can do for us, and he's proving to be very useful in fixing up a few things around the house. That's all!'

Emerald smirked at her, and put her head on one side, knowingly.

'I think you should make some detailed enquiries about your young man, before you allow him the free run of your house. That's all I'm saying.'

Margaret shook her head impatiently.

'What are you implying? That he's a thief! That he's a rogue! I can assure you, Mister Blood is quite transparent, quite above board. I trust him implicitly.'

'Well, that's nice for him. I'd keep him away from Jane, though, if I were you. It could work out rather unpleasantly for everyone involved.'

'If you've got something to say, Emerald, just come out with it. Why keep on making these vague insinuations without backing them up with some concrete facts?'

'I keep my own counsel,' smiled Emerald, mysteriously. 'I have the knack of ferreting out dark secrets wherever I go, but until I have the actual proof, then I won't make those accusations openly. We all know that's the way to end up in court.'

'You must have a very devious mind, Emerald, if you can find any fault with our Mister Blood. He has little or no knowledge of the proprieties, I must admit. He's ingenuous at best, ignorant at worst, but a thoroughly nice young man, nevertheless.'

Emerald pursed her lips, and looked disappointed. She had hoped to invoke a greater reaction than this from her distant cousin.

'Well anyway. He may just be after old Theodore's fortune. Haven't found it yet, have you?'

'No, Emerald, we haven't found it yet, no! But I'll be sure to notify you the moment it turns up.'

'You can be as sarcastic as you like, Margaret. But I at least *do* know where it is to be found. It's amazing what a little bit of research in the right places can do.'

'I'm sure that if you knew where to find it, you would have snaffled it and been gone by now. A hundred and twenty years has failed to turn it up. What makes you think that you know where it is after all this time, when so many before you have failed?'

Emerald wiggled her shoulders in self-satisfaction, and smirked again.

'Because I read the papers, Margaret! I read the papers. Not only the Australian ones, but also the South African ones, that's why. I've spent ten years researching old Theodore, and I know every move he made. In actual fact, you could call me an expert on the life of Theodore Schuman.'

'It still hasn't turned up the three hundred thousand pounds that disappeared. Well, three hundred thousand that we know of… there may have been more.'

'Oh no! Three hundred and fifteen thousand it was. I have the bank records and withdrawals for that time, so I know. It's all in black and white.'

'Okay! If you know so much, Emerald, why don't you let us all in on the secret, and we'll all go quarters. You, me, Ingrid and Jane! How's that?'

'Oh no, I'm not going to give up all my secrets as easily as that. Perhaps if you'd like to see a solicitor and draw up an agreement, we'll see what can be done. But any agreement would have to include me on the title deeds for this house. That's only fair.'

Margaret scowled at her.

'You can go to hell, Emerald!'

Then she slammed the door in her face.

Chapter Five

Graham arrived back at the hotel at eight thirty. He proceeded into the little dining room there and ordered a breakfast of bacon, sausages, eggs and toast, and had two cups of coffee to wash it down. He was famished after missing the previous evening's meal, and had a bowl of cereal while waiting for it to be cooked. The publican's wife, Joan, finally delivered his meal on a tray, and made a great fuss of laying it out for him on the table. She was a few years younger than her husband, and had a bit of a roving eye. Graham sat back to give her access, and was startled when she fluttered her eyelashes at him, leaned across him and pressed her breasts against his shoulder.

'Oh, er, thank you Mrs. Evans. That's very nice, thank you! I'll sort it out from there.'

'I wouldn't think of it, Mister Blood. You're my guest here, and I wouldn't have any of my guests saying the service wasn't up to scratch. And do call me Joan! I like my young men to know I'm accessible. It's no good standing on ceremony in a little place like Heaven's Ridge.'

Graham looked her directly in the eye, and noted that one of her eyebrows was raised. She flashed a brilliant smile that hit him like a physical assault. It said, *'just ask me, that's all you have to do...'*

'I'll certainly bear that in mind,' he said, and smiled back.

Joan seemed satisfied and took her tray, then teetered back to the kitchen on her stiletto heels. Graham's eyes followed her, and he noted how tightly her belt was pulled in, accentuating her rather heavy hour-glass figure. He thought of Evans, then shook his head. The man must have something…

By nine-fifteen he was heading up the road towards the house. Across from the pub he saw a woman with gardening gloves on, standing in her front garden and taking especial notice of him. He hesitated, then gave her a friendly wave. She raised one hand, tentatively, then lowered it again. What was it with the women in this place?

The only detour he made was to the service bay of the mechanic's, where he went into the boot of his car and retrieved a tool box which he took with him to Heaven's Ridge. By the time he was approaching the front step of the house it was almost nine-thirty. He didn't have to knock, the door opened as he raised his hand.

'You're late,' Margaret snapped, as she stepped aside to allow him entry.

'Yes, I know,' he said, breezily. 'It was such a lovely morning that I decided to go for a walk on the beach. There's a magnificent view from down there.'

'I'm well aware of the view, Mister Blood. We had an arrangement.'

Graham sighed, mentally. He knew she wouldn't be able to leave it alone.

'Loosen up, Margaret. I'm on holiday! Dock me half an hour if you like, but let's just keep it informal.'

'*Miss* Margaret!' she snapped.

'Oh, that's right. We mustn't relax our etiquette, must we? People will think we're having a jolly affair on the side. That wouldn't do, would it?'

'It certainly wouldn't, Mister Blood! What on earth has got into you this morning?' Margaret said, indignantly.

'The joy of life,' Graham grinned. 'The marvels of the universe. The uniqueness of the planet we live on, and the fact that today is the first day of the rest of our lives.'

Margaret took a step back and looked at him, puzzled.

'We don't go in for levity in the mornings at Heaven's Ridge, Mister Blood. It's most unsettling. Please follow me through to the garden.'

They walked along the passageway, through the end door and went out into the garden as they'd done the day before. Ingrid was standing a little way down the garden, looking somewhat sheepish. Graham began to walk towards her.

'Ah, Ingrid, my sweet one. Isn't this a day for falling in love... don't you think?' he said mischievously.

Ingrid looked from one side to the other, to make sure it was she he was talking to, not some spectre. Then she blushed and stammered a reply.

'I really don't... Oh! I see! You're pulling my leg.'

Graham grinned at her and looked positively boyish. Margaret was standing on the lawn looking stern and unforgiving, but Ingrid suddenly began to laugh.

'Oh, don't worry, Margaret. It's just a young man's idea of a joke.'

'Well, joke or no joke, he has work to do. Please don't allow him to be side-tracked,

Ingrid.' She then turned and walked stiffly back into the house.

On the other side of the lawn there was a swing set, with two old, rusty swings, hanging from chains. Graham made his way over to these and sat down on one. Ingrid followed slowly, looking dreadfully unsure of herself.

'Come and sit down, Ingrid. We'll go for a soar.'

Ingrid sneaked a glimpse back at the house, then, once sure that Margaret had disappeared, walked gingerly over and sat on the next swing.

'Won't our clothes get dreadfully dirty,' she said, looking at the rust on her hands.

'Nothing that won't wash off,' he replied cheerfully. He pushed off and began to swing back and forth, encouraging her to do the same.

'Come on, give it a start, it won't propel itself,' he enjoined.

She smiled mysteriously, and sneaked a sideways look at him. Then she pushed off, very tentatively at first, then with more vigor, smiling as her efforts yielded fruit.

'You've almost caught up to me, Ingrid. That will never do,' he called out, increasing his efforts. Ingrid was openly laughing by this time, and the two swings were creaking and rattling fit to burst. Suddenly she put her feet down and dragged to a stop.

'It's going to break… I know it's going to break,' she huffed, out of breath from the exertion and from laughing. Graham slowed down and stopped.

'It would take more than little you to break these old chains,' he said, inspecting the thick old chain rings. Then he reached over and took hold of her hand, turning it over and inspecting the palm. She was covered in rust stains. Ingrid sat there, deathly quiet, her other hand clutching at her throat. All she could think of was that a man was holding her by the hand.

'Disgusting,' he said, flippantly. 'Putrid!' he continued, turning her hand first one way then the other. Then inexplicably he bent forward and kissed the palm of her hand.

'There, that should fix it.' He looked up and grinned his boyish grin, and she suddenly laughed despite herself. She sounded like a young girl, not a middle aged woman in her forty-third year. Graham noticed that she was flushed, and that this extra pressure through the capillaries made the lines and creases in her face disappear. She suddenly looked ten years younger.

'Margaret thought you might be able to do something with these swings,' Ingrid said, getting up. They've been neglected for years, but it would be good if you could restore them to a serviceable state. A bit of white paint, or something.'

'I'll do better than that, madam, I'll de-rust the lot and then undercoat them properly and have them gleaming and white in no time.'

Ingrid looked sceptical, as if she thought these rusty old swings could never be restored to such a pristine condition. Graham noted her expression.

'You don't believe me! If I say I'm going to do something, I do it! Now away with you woman. How can a man develop empathy with a wire brush when he is distracted by such a vision of feminine beauty.'

Ingrid's jaw dropped, then she giggled. Before he knew it she was hurrying back towards the house, her shoulders shaking, this time, with silent laughter.

II

Graham had been working on the swings for just over an hour when a gate in the fence opened on the eastern side, and a woman in a long white dress came limping through. He looked up and smiled, then saw that the limp was more pronounced than he'd thought so hurried over to give her a hand.

'What happened? Did you fall over?' he said, supporting her by the arm.

'And you are?' she enquired, rather haughtily. There seemed to be a bit of Margaret in this one.

'Blood! Graham Blood,' he replied, holding out his hand. She shook it.

He helped her to hobble over to an old garden seat, and made sure that she was safely sat down.

'I'm Jane Wiltshire,' she said. 'I take it that you're the odd-job man everyone's talking about!'

'Everyone?' said Graham. 'I didn't think there were that many 'everyone's' around here.'

'Oh, you know what I mean. Margaret, Ingrid, Emerald from up the road… she was here earlier. Old Evans at the pub, and his wife, Joan!'

As she said the name 'Joan', she raised an eyebrow and peered into his face with a quizzical expression.

'You do know *'Joan'*, don't you?'

'Well, she served my breakfast this morning, if you can call that knowing someone. Otherwise I've never seen her before.'

'But you *do* know Emerald. You *must* know Emerald!'

'Never heard of her,' said Graham, shaking his head. 'Who's Emerald?' He seemed genuinely mystified.

'She lives opposite the hotel in the main street. She's usually out there early, doing her garden.'

'Oh, that one! I gave her a wave as I was coming up here today. But I don't know her... no.' Graham looked puzzled now. This one certainly didn't live by Margaret's precepts.

'Well, she certainly thinks she knows you. She made a point of coming up here this morning to brag about it. But that's Emerald.'

Graham shook his head.

'Like I said...never heard of her. Now look... did you sprain your ankle or what? That looked like a nasty limp. Would you like me to take a look at it?'

Jane looked at him with a bored expression on her face.

'How prosaic! Oh well, if you must...'

She thrust her leg out and watched his face. Graham looked down, then started back in shock.

Jane made a point of looking down also, then pulled a face.

'Oh dear… worse than I thought! It must have fallen off.'

Graham looked in horror at the base of her leg. The foot was missing altogether. Over the stump where the ankle should have been was a round leather cover, something like a horseshoe. It was this that she put her weight on. No wonder she limped!

'Do you enjoy shocking people,' said Graham, somewhat angrily. If it was a joke, he thought it in very poor taste.

'Do you find it repulsive, Mister Blood?'

Her expression was sardonic.

'No, I don't find it repulsive. It just gave me a shock, that's all! You should have warned me!'

'Oh, but then it would lose all its entertainment value.'

'I'd hardly call it entertaining!'

'Not entertainment for you, dear boy… but for me! Oh yes, I find it very entertaining. The look on your face! Dear me! Precious!'

Graham stared at her as if she were some sort of monster. And yet she was beautiful, incredibly beautiful. She had high crafted cheekbones and full lips, and eyebrows that arched to fix a perpetual look of astonishment on her face. Either that, or superciliousness, he couldn't work out which.

He was silent for a moment, not really knowing how to continue this bizarre conversation. She seemed highly amused, and sat there fanning herself with her hand. Noting his discomfort, she laughed.

'Don't worry. My hand won't fall off. All my other bits are fixed.'

'You really do revel in this, don't you?' said Graham, annoyed. 'And I always thought that people with infirmities were sensitive about their problems.'

'It was a long time ago, Mister Blood. At least give me credit for not sitting around all day bemoaning my fate. When something like this happens, you just have to get on with it. That's what I'm doing.'

There was a long silence.

'What exactly happened? Or is that too personal a question.'

Jane looked at him with renewed interest.

'I can see you've been tutored in the matter of etiquette by my aunt Margaret. Never ask personal questions, keep it formal. Don't get involved! Control your emotions; all that sort of tripe.'

Graham nodded.

'Well that should give you a clue then. What sort of person wants to avoid answering personal questions? I'll answer it for you… a person with something to hide.'

'So… your aunt was in some way responsible for… that!'

Graham nodded down at her leg, which was still thrust out in his line of sight.

'Not in some way; *totally* responsible. I was eleven years old, Mister Blood. And like any other eleven-year old girl I was beginning to rebel. I used to travel to school every day, mix with other children, listen to outrageous ideas, blasphemous theories, evil doctrines of the wicked world out there. I brought disgusting concepts home, like pyjama parties, little girl sleep-overs, hero worship, and worst of all, I believed my teacher told the truth while my aunt lied. I would question her authority with… *but my teacher says!* This was totally unacceptable. One day I came home and said I was going to run away.'

Jane stared into the middle distance, as if she could still see clearly the events of those days, fourteen years before.

'I had a horse. Not a pony, like other kids had. A horse! It was too big for me, but their reasoning was that I'd grow out of a pony, whereas a horse would last me until I grew up. It used to be stabled on the other side of that fence over there. There was a large paddock for it to run free in, and a stable where it would spend cold nights. In the stable was a stall, just big enough to fence him in, and he hated it! Whenever he was put into his stall he would try to buck and stamp and kick the door open. I don't blame him, actually. It must have been like a prison to him. A bit like living at Heaven's Ridge.'

She paused, to catch her breath, and to give greater emphasis to her story.

'When I said I was going to run away, I was beaten, and locked in the punishment room. I was stubborn though, and determined not to be cowed. When I think back, I'm quite proud of how I was then. I had spirit, and no one could crush it. My spirit was indomitable! I went to school the following week and told my teacher I had been locked in a room over the weekend, and what for, and my teacher sent a note home. I don't know what it said, but it threw Margaret into a rage. I remember her storming around the house, shouting at the top of her voice, and saying things like… *'no little brat is going to question my authority.'* I have a faint memory of the word 'bastard' being used, also 'illegitimate', 'mongrel', 'love-child', and 'foundling.'

The following weekend, Margaret took me over to the stables. Rob Roy, that was my horse, had been locked in his stall for an hour or so at this stage, and was kicking up a fuss. Margaret told me that we were going to let him out for a while. When we got there, I stood outside the stall door, and tried to calm him down. Margaret came up behind me and threw me on the floor, then pushed my leg underneath the door. Well, you can imagine what happened. Rob Roy reared and stamped and pounded and kicked and crushed my foot to a bloody pulp. I was lucky I didn't lose the rest of my leg. As it was, the doctors said it would have to come off. There wasn't an unbroken bone in my foot, and most of them were crushed and fractured in numerous places. So off it came. There was no more talk of running away after that, nor even of walking away. I suppose I could have said… *'when I grow up I'm going to hobble away...'* but I fancied keeping at least one foot intact, and so, I suppose, she did manage to crush my spirit after all. I'm still here, aren't I? And I'm twenty five years old.'

Graham had stood up halfway through the narrative, and was now looking down at her in a sort of fascinated horror. He wanted to speak, but there were no words available to describe what he felt about such an inhuman act. He could only stand there with his mouth open, and attempt to form words that wouldn't come. Jane ignored him, and carried on.

'Of course, there was no more school for me after that. I was tutored at home, and all my little friends grew up and forgot all about me. I became just that little kid that had an accident with a horse. The saddest thing was that my horse had to go. They knocked down the stable, and now, whenever I get within fifty yards of a horse I go into shock. I experience this blind terror from somewhere in my subconscious, that would put me into a catatonic trance if I were ever forced to stand next to one. My conscious reason tells me it wasn't the horse's fault. My subconscious goes into spasm. So that's the story of my footless foot. Can you handle it?'

'No – I don't think I can,' said Graham, a quaver in his voice. He looked down at his hands, and they were shaking. Whether from anger or shock, he couldn't determine. But he couldn't take his eyes off Jane's stump, and the sight of that almost made him throw up.

'So now you know! Do you also know what you're here for,' Jane said, trying to lighten it a little.

'Odd jobs,' Graham mumbled. 'Just a few odd jobs. There's a lot of things need fixing around here.'

Jane laughed out loud, and continued to laugh.

'Oh, you don't know the half of it. There's plenty to fix all right. Take me for a start.'

Graham looked at her in surprise.

'What do you mean by that? If you're talking about your leg…'

'No, of course not! No, your prime purpose here is to deflower me. Didn't you know that? A good-looking young fellow like yourself! Men like you are in short supply around here. No doubt the old hags have come up with this plan to get me impregnated, so we can carry on the family tree. I'm the last, you see. And our cousin Emerald is a spinster and past it as well. No doubt you've been out and about in the world, deflowering virgins as you go, and in their understanding you'll just need a little push, and whatever it is that men do to women will be done, and I'll bring forth the next generation. After you've done the deed, of course, you'll get the push. You'll be on your way! We have no need of men around here, messing with Margaret's iron rules of behaviour, and questioning her authority.'

Graham stood back, his mouth agape.

'I hardly know what to say! That's about the most forthright thing I've ever heard issue from the mouth of a woman. Especially from a...' he hesitated; 'a virgin!'

'Don't you believe that I'm a virgin?'

'After taking in the local regime, I wouldn't have any quarrel with that. But don't I get any consideration here? Doesn't it matter what *I* want in this scheme of things?'

'Not at all,' Jane laughed. 'Does it matter what a Praying Mantis wants when he mounts the female? Of course not! As he completes the act of copulation she turns around and bites his head off.'

'So I'm just to be a means to an end,' said Graham, shaking his head. 'And who came up with this great scheme?'

'Well, I'm not actually privy to the inner councils of this household, but from what I've picked up it was Margaret's idea, and Ingrid went along. God forbid that Theodore should be left with no descendants. What would happen to Heaven's Ridge? It beggars the thought.'

'But Heaven's Ridge is merely a house, for god's sake. Just a house! Not that much of an extraordinary one either. Someone will no doubt come along and buy it, sooner or later.'

Jane shook her head. Then she shook it again, most emphatically.

'Heaven's Ridge is not just a house. That's where you're wrong, Mister Blood. Heaven's Ridge is much more than that. Maybe if you're here long enough, you will begin to appreciate just how much more. But then I'd have to kill you.'

Jane laughed at the sudden expression on his face, and Graham stared back, trying to work out just how serious that remark was really meant to be.

Chapter Six

'What are you looking so foolishly happy about,' said Margaret, when Ingrid returned to the kitchen.

Ingrid straightened her face and looked ingenuously at her older sister.

'Happy? What's wrong with looking happy, Margaret? Could it be something that we've forgotten to be in this house? Happy!'

'Any excess of that type of emotion is bad for you,' said Margaret. 'I find it very suspicious! You're usually moping around the place giving me dark looks, and now, here you are, bubbling over with yourself.'

'Maybe I just needed a tonic, Margaret. That young man's a real tonic! He has the ability to make all your worries seem so trivial. I think we take ourselves far too seriously, do you know that?'

'Life is a serious business, Ingrid. And so is reputation… you should remember that! There's many a slip 'twixt the cup and the lip.'

Ingrid sat down at the table and looked at her hands. They were still covered in brown rust.

'I get so tired of your litany of aphorisms, Margaret. Do you think you could ever get through a paragraph without attempting to point out some self-evident truth? It always comes across as hectoring.'

'There's nothing wrong with maintaining a highly moral stance. In an evil world, it's the only thing that stands between us and the beasts of the field.'

'That's exactly what I mean,' said Ingrid, staring at Margaret with intense dislike. 'Two minutes with you, and I'm starting to feel depressed already. I was in a wonderful mood when I came in through that door.'

'Yes… but ask yourself why! You're allowing emotions of the moment to carry you away. I've told you before; it's the gross emotional nature that carries us to perdition. You spend ten minutes with a personable young man and he sets your heart all a-flutter. Where's your self-control, Ingrid? Where's your sense of pride?'

'God, you're boring Margaret! Have I really spent the last forty-two years putting up with this… voluntarily?'

Margaret looked hurt. She picked up a knife and started chopping carrots into rounds.

'You know where the door is, Ingrid. If you think you can find a better world out there, go to it! It won't affect me in any way whatsoever. I shall still be here, carrying the Family Standard so to speak.'

Ingrid laughed, a short staccato sound.

'But for how long? You know and I know that it's coming to the end of the line. There is no more family, Margaret. There never will be.'

Margaret put down her knife, and stared at Ingrid across the table.

'How can you be so sure of that?'

Ingrid stared back.

'What do you mean by that?'

'If you only listened to me, occasionally, you might actually get to understand what's going on. Didn't you hear what I said to you, in the hotel yesterday? I asked if this Mister Blood was for Jane! She's only twenty-eight, you know.'

'What do you mean... for Jane? He hasn't even met Jane yet. You deliberately kept her out of the way yesterday, locked her in her room. I know, because I went by and checked the door.'

'I'm well aware of that. But you're wrong about him not meeting Jane. He's out there with her now!'

Ingrid started, then leant forward over the table, glowering at her sister intently.

'God, you're twisted! What's the big idea? I arranged for him to come and do a few odd jobs around the place, and then move on. What devious little scheme have you got worked out this time? Mister Blood is not going to be another Will Shire!'

'I never suggested he was,' said Margaret, smiling privately to herself. 'But nevertheless, he will do admirably for our purposes. All we have to do is to maneuver them together a few times, and give them a little space, and the inevitable will come about. That's the one thing about man's coarse nature that we can rely on.'

'But that's the most horrible thing I've ever heard! You talk about others, Margaret, but you've got a mind like a cesspit. What makes you think that our Mister Blood will even take to Jane. She's so flippant and superficial that she'll probably put him off. And anyway, I don't think Mister Blood's like that at all. He would have to be in love with a woman before engaging in carnal relations with her.'

Margaret shook her head, and tutted to herself.

'Ingrid... Ingrid... Always so naïve! It's easy to see that you have never really grasped the downright wickedness of this world. It's in man's inherent nature, dear girl, to sully and defile everything he touches. The one advantage in this is that he also produces children, as a sort of consolation prize. But they come as merely a by-blow to the main event, which is man's inordinate desire to invade a woman's personal space.'

Ingrid shook her head violently.

'That's not true! There are a lot of men out there who desire children, and they make good fathers as well. They don't all run around with other women and leave their wives on the scrapheap. There are some very good men out there!'

'Oh yes! You know this from personal experience, do you? You've obviously met a lot of these idealistic gentlemen on your many travels in the world. Perhaps you have had long discussions on the subject?'

Ingrid blushed, and dropped her head.

'I don't care! I don't think Mister Blood is like that… and I don't think you have any right to maneuver him into a situation which might prove embarrassing to him.'

Margaret slammed her fist on the table and made Ingrid jump.

'Now you listen to me. You know very well that it is our duty to make sure that Theodore's descendants don't peter out. He has provided for this family for over a hundred years. True, the greater part of his fortune disappeared at his death, but his shares and other investments have provided for four generations, and we ourselves have lived more than comfortably on the proceeds, all our lives. Why do you think Emerald is so keen to get under our roof? She wants the income that comes with it!'

Ingrid frowned, and looked away.

'I don't care about Emerald. She's never going to have children, anyway. She's too old.'

'Exactly! And so are we! Let's face it, Ingrid, this is our only chance. If we want to have someone to leave this place to, we have to help Jane get pregnant. For some reason best known to himself, the good lord made that impossible without the intervention of a male of the species. We have our male in Mister Blood! We're going to have to use him to bring about the desired result. I've decided that it would be better if we offered him the guest room for the rest of his stay here. We can make some excuse, like it's too far to be lugging his toolbox back and forwards between here and the hotel.'

'What if he refuses,' said Ingrid, hopefully.

'He won't refuse! I want you to use your influence – he obviously likes you – by inviting him to dinner tonight. I shall cook up a nice roast, and you can go down the road later and bring in some wine. A Queen Adelaide Riesling would go down well.'

'Gentlemen often prefer spirits,' Ingrid sulked.

'In that case it will be your job to find out what sort of spirits he prefers, and get in the appropriate mixers. If we can soften him up with a good meal and a belly full of alcohol, it will be easier to work on his carnal nature. He only has to do it once... or so I'm given to understand, anyway. Perhaps we'd better try and keep him going for a week, just to make sure. Then once that's over, we can tip him out the door.'

'You realize this might blow up in your face. What if he decides he wants to take her away with him? What if he falls in love? He might decide to stay on, indefinitely, and that wouldn't suit you at all, would it?'

'There's no question of that. And there will be no question of Jane leaving, either. We've kept her with us this long, we can make it impossible for her to leave. Once he's gone, there will be no reason for her to go, especially if she's pregnant.'

Ingrid stood up. She looked suddenly tired and worn.

'I don't like it… I'll tell you that now! I think we're doing poor Mister Blood a grave disservice. But I suppose we have to suppress our own feelings in the matter for the future good of the family, so I'll do it. But I don't like it.'

She turned and left the room, and if Margaret had been especially observant, she would have seen two small tears edging out of the corners of Ingrid's eyes.

II

'I saw you this morning, through that gate over there! You were standing at the opening, looking down at me on the beach.'

'What makes you think I was looking at you?' said Jane.

She was sitting on the lawn, watching Graham attack the swings with a wire brush. Luckily the wind was blowing in the other direction, otherwise she would have been covered in a fine coating of rust by now.

Graham ceased his attack and looked at her. Except for the footless leg, thrust out on the grass, she would have made a pretty picture. That missing foot spoiled the image. Despite her fine features, Graham couldn't help thinking that there was something not quite right with Jane Wiltshire. There was an innate arrogance about her that she didn't even try to hide. Perhaps that was a compensatory device to make up for her deformity. If you can't defend, attack!'

'Do you always question everything, even the obvious?' he said.

'I'd hardly say it was obvious. I could have been doing anything.'

'Yes, you could have been. But what you were actually doing was standing in that gateway, looking down at me.'

Jane looked away, and affected a look of supercilious disdain. The wind flicked at her hair, which was straight and blonde. From the waist up she looked like a model on the cover of Vogue magazine.

'I haven't exactly spent my life fawning over men,' she remarked. 'Even if I'd wanted to, which I didn't, Margaret would have seen to it that no opportunities arose for that. She rules this house with an iron fist!'

Graham got stuck into one of the seats with the wire brush.

'So I'm given to believe. But from what I've seen of Ingrid, she can give as good as she gets.'

Jane nodded, and continued staring into space.

'Yes, well… she had a good teacher. No one could live with Margaret for as long as those two have been together, without some of it at least, rubbing off. They're like chalk and cheese those two. It wouldn't surprise me if the whole thing erupted into a bloodbath one night, the way they talk to each other. When they get arguing – usually about the most trivial things – you'd swear that the knives are going to suddenly appear, and there'll be the most terrible slashing and stabbing and screaming until one or the other, or both, are lying on the floor in pools of blood.'

'You have a real *penchant* for the melodramatic, don't you,' said Graham, smiling. 'Is that because you lead a boring life?'

Jane suddenly looked at him, a gleam of amusement in her eyes.

'You think that, do you? That my life is boring! I can assure you, that's the last thing my life is. You see, I'm a student of human nature. I watch, listen and learn! There's not a lot that gets by me, I can assure you! I can usually predict behaviours in advance, given a fixed set of circumstances, and a basic knowledge of the persons involved.' She was silent for a moment, then said, seemingly irrelevantly, 'I'm good at jigsaws, too!'

Graham looked at her, and nodded.

'So life is a jigsaw. You just have to put the pieces together.'

'Not so simple as that,' she smiled. 'You have to work out where the pieces fit first, then put the jigsaw together, otherwise you don't get the complete picture.'

'Now we're wandering into areas of semantics, and I was never very good at that,' he grinned. 'I still say you were looking down at me from that garden gate this morning. What else would you be looking at?'

'If you've got five minutes, maybe I can show you,' said Jane, struggling up onto one foot. She swayed there for a moment, until Graham threw down the wire brush, dusted his hands together and hurried over to support her. She put her arm around his shoulder, and began to hobble towards the gate on the cliff side of the garden.

He hadn't seen it before because it was located around behind the sheds, further down the garden. He hadn't been that far before. As they walked he was very aware of her hip against his.

Each time she put her stump down on the ground to walk, it threw her hip sideways and into his leg. One leg must have been three inches shorter than the other.

She looked at him, close up.

'Does that turn you on,' she remarked, unabashed.

He flashed her a look that said he was not amused.

'I refuse to answer loaded questions! For once, I'm in agreement with your aunt Margaret. There are some things that should not be spoken out loud.'

Jane laughed and ruffled his hair.

'You really are a bit of a prat, aren't you,' she said. 'Are you afraid of me?'

'Not afraid, no! But I'm always a bit reticent where it comes to the predatory female.'

She smiled at him, mysteriously, and hobbled on a few more paces.

'I'd say, Mister Blood, if I wanted to use the modern idiom, that you've got tickets on yourself. You have this sneaking suspicion that all women are just waiting for the opportunity to fall at your feet. If that's the case, I think it's about time you realized that you're not *that* much of a catch!'

Graham stopped suddenly, and grinned at her.

'Is that so? I thought I spent my life wandering hither and thither, deflowering virgins – according to you!'

'No! I didn't say according to me. I said according to Margaret's strange, myopic view of the role of men in this world. She thinks that's all you're good for.'

'Well that's very reassuring, I must say. Positively complimentary, I don't think!'

They both grinned, and hobbled up to the gate.

It was an old wooden affair, very rickety by the look of it, and Jane leant back against the fence as he attempted to open it.

'It's a bit sticky. You have to really wrench at it to get it open,' she said.

Graham tugged on it a couple of times, and finally it gave, and swung open. He walked forward into the opening and looked across at the beach, so far below. He'd only stood there for a few seconds when he felt a push in the back, and he jack-knifed forward, bent at the waist, and found himself staring straight down the side of the cliff. For an agonizing moment he thought he was going to topple forward and fall head first, but then he felt a restraining grip on his collar, and he just hung there, looking down over a hundred feet to the rocks at the bottom. He was suddenly seized with an overwhelming attack of vertigo, and the world spun in front of his eyes.

'Get me back, for chrisesake...' he yelled, swinging his arms for balance.

Jane yanked him back by the collar, and he fell backwards, landing in a heap on the grass, three feet from the edge. He fell onto his back and covered his face with his hands. Jane leant side on against the gatepost and looked down at him, sardonically.

'Life's so boring here, isn't it,' she said, amused.

Graham lay on his back, getting his breath back. His head was still spinning and his heart was going into palpitations.

'You bloody mad bitch,' he yelled, once he had recovered himself. He was really angry, and somewhat embarrassed at his display of weakness. He jumped up to his feet and stood hanging onto the open gate. 'That's bloody dangerous. What are you trying to prove?'

Jane seemed unperturbed. She looked out over the distant beach, and then took a step forward and peered down the cliff. She spoke softly.

'I thought you might be interested in experiencing my mother's last few seconds in this life, before she plunged over the edge and was smashed to death on the rocks down there.'

Graham shrank back against the door, and went as white as a ghost.

'I don't believe you,' he said. 'You're lying!'

Jane raised her arm and pointed to the lintel of the gate. It was old and worn, and had been painted in a dark green fence paint. But scratched into the timber, and clearly visible were the words, *'Helen's Leap'*.

Jane turned away, and hobbled back into the garden, then stood with her back to him.

'Don't believe me! It makes no odds to me. But it's true! She came out here at ten o'clock one morning, and after one last, despairing look at the world, took a swan dive over the cliff. I was only a few days old. You see, she thought she'd been left in the lurch, and the shame was too much for her to bear.'

Graham struggled to slam the gate on that view, and as it closed pounded his fist on the gate. Then he rested his forehead against it, and shut his eyes in horror at some thought of his own.

'I was told she died in childbirth! Everybody seems to think she died in childbirth!'

'Nobody thinks that! They all know! That's just the story they trot out for strangers. If you don't believe me you can check it out in the records of the coroner's court. *'Death by Misadventure'* they called it. So much nicer than suicide, don't you think? Takes the weight of all that blame off everyone's shoulders. There was no proof that it was a suicide, of course. I believe there was a note, but Margaret burned it – or so Ingrid told me, years later. It wouldn't surprise me, knowing Margaret. She probably played the sinner's card for all it was worth, terrorised my mother with hellfire and damnation for straying from the path of the righteous. That's what she's like! Then, when she'd driven her crazy with fear, she showed Will Shire the door, and told my mother that he'd taken off, deserted her. No doubt she rubbed it in, told her she'd got her just desserts for being a slut, a hussy, and that she would now forever be a fallen woman. Faced with that for the rest of her life, I'm not surprised she took the easy way out.'

Graham was ashen faced as he turned back to her.

'Easy? I wouldn't call that easy,' he replied, quietly. 'It makes me feel sick just to think about it.'

'Anyway,' Jane said, more brightly. 'Now do you believe me when I say I wasn't there this morning just to look at you? That gateway does have other associations for me, other purposes than for just spying on the tourists wandering along the beach.'

Graham looked back at the gate, and shook his head.

'It looks downright dangerous to me. If I were you I'd be boarding it up. It's just an accident, waiting to happen.'

'Accident?' Jane said. She almost snapped the word. 'Accident? There are no accidents at Heaven's Ridge! Everything that happens here is planned, down to the last detail. There is no room for error. After all, we have all the time in the world up here, to conspire, plan, scheme and deliberate!'

At that moment they were interrupted by the form of Ingrid, hurrying over from the house.

'Margaret and I would like to invite you to dinner tonight, Mister Blood... that is, if you haven't anything else planned.' She shot Jane a withering look on the side, then turned back to Graham, and smiled.

'Oh, that's very nice of you, Ingrid. Certainly, I'd love to come to dinner.'

Ingrid smiled again, then turned and went back to the house.

'Everything that happens here is planned...' Jane whispered, watching Ingrid's retreating form. Graham looked at her and smiled, grimly.

'Well if you weren't *'planning'* to look at me on the beach this morning, just what were you *'planning'* to do?'

Jane threw her head back, and looked at him from underneath her arched eyebrows.

'I was *'planning'*... to jump,' she said.

Chapter Seven

By six o'clock that evening, Graham had completed his work with the wire brush, and had applied a plentiful coat of red oxide to the swings, taken his leave of the sisters and returned to the hotel for a shower. On the way he had been waylaid by a brimming Emerald Schuman, who bobbed up out of her garden like a hobgoblin and pointed a long finger in his direction.

'You're Elizabeth's, aren't you? Your grandmother, I mean!'

Graham had stopped in his tracks, and wandered over to the little fence that skirted her property.

'I'm sorry,' he said. 'I don't think I know you.'

'Emerald,' she said, proffering a pudgy hand, 'Emerald Schuman. I met your grandmother once, back in... let me see, it must have been in 1955. They were over here on holiday, and just happened to be staying in Moonta. That's where I come from you know! Moonta! My father Hayden was working in a local garage there, and John Blood came in to get a part for his car. Even then, he would never have twigged if Elizabeth hadn't shown up suddenly, to remind her husband to get a punctured tyre fixed. She had Christopher with her, your father. He was only ten at the time. Hayden recognized her immediately, even though the last time he'd met his cousin was at Heaven's Ridge, on a visit there in 1943. Elizabeth had only been fourteen at the time of that first meeting, but he recognized her the moment he saw her, twelve years later. And of course, he'd already heard about her disappearance in 1944. She was pregnant, wasn't she? I always said that was why she took off.'

Emerald paused for breath, while Graham stared at her, with a seemingly pensive look. He'd gone somewhat grey in the face.

'But it was the surname that gave you away. There's not that many Bloods around you know. As soon as Evans mentioned your name, I knew there was a mystery there. You've come over from the west, haven't you? No doubt your grandmother filled your head up with tales about old Theodore, and you've come over to suss it out – am I right?'

She waited expectantly for a reply, but Graham just looked at her in disgust, and turned to walk away.

'That makes you my third cousin, once removed, you realize,' she shouted after him. 'And it makes you Jane's second cousin. You remember that! Second cousins! You've got a touch of the bad blood in you too.'

Graham kept walking, and disappeared through the front door of the hotel. Once inside, he went straight up to his room, shut the door behind him and punched the wall. Of all the coincidences that could have possibly happened, he hadn't foreseen that one.

Emerald Schuman! Going to his bed, he reached down and pulled out a briefcase that he'd hidden, out of sight. Snapping the locks open, he rummaged through it and pulled out a large chart, made up like a family tree. He spread it out on the bed and perused it carefully. In the bottom right hand corner, he saw the name Emerald Schuman. She was right... she was his distant cousin! The chart read as follows.

Schuman Family Tree

Theodore Schuman	m.	Ethel Williams
b. 1832 at Hamburg		b. 1838 at Melbourne
d. 1883 at Kimberley, S. Africa		d. 1874 at Heaven's Ridge
(Syphilis)		m. 1865 at Bendigo, Victoria

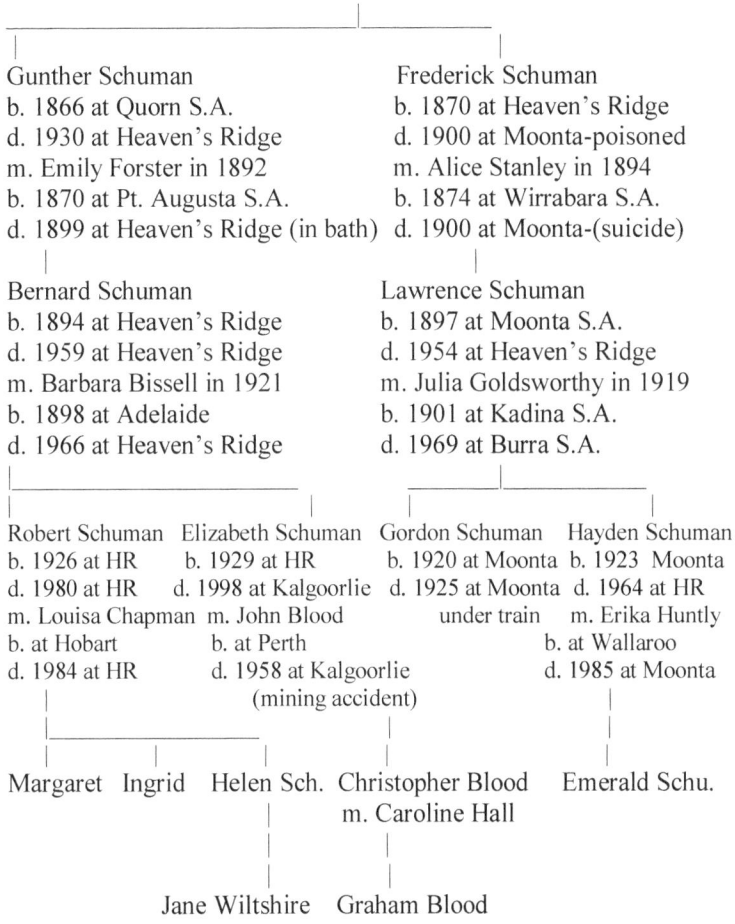

Gunther Schuman
b. 1866 at Quorn S.A.
d. 1930 at Heaven's Ridge
m. Emily Forster in 1892
b. 1870 at Pt. Augusta S.A.
d. 1899 at Heaven's Ridge (in bath)

Frederick Schuman
b. 1870 at Heaven's Ridge
d. 1900 at Moonta-poisoned
m. Alice Stanley in 1894
b. 1874 at Wirrabara S.A.
d. 1900 at Moonta-(suicide)

Bernard Schuman
b. 1894 at Heaven's Ridge
d. 1959 at Heaven's Ridge
m. Barbara Bissell in 1921
b. 1898 at Adelaide
d. 1966 at Heaven's Ridge

Lawrence Schuman
b. 1897 at Moonta S.A.
d. 1954 at Heaven's Ridge
m. Julia Goldsworthy in 1919
b. 1901 at Kadina S.A.
d. 1969 at Burra S.A.

Robert Schuman
b. 1926 at HR
d. 1980 at HR
m. Louisa Chapman
b. at Hobart
d. 1984 at HR

Elizabeth Schuman
b. 1929 at HR
d. 1998 at Kalgoorlie
m. John Blood
b. at Perth
d. 1958 at Kalgoorlie
(mining accident)

Gordon Schuman
b. 1920 at Moonta
d. 1925 at Moonta
under train

Hayden Schuman
b. 1923 Moonta
d. 1964 at HR
m. Erika Huntly
b. at Wallaroo
d. 1985 at Moonta

Margaret   Ingrid   Helen Sch.   Christopher Blood   Emerald Schu.
                                     m. Caroline Hall

Jane Wiltshire   Graham Blood

Graham perused the sheet, and bit his lip. This was a bad time for this to come out. If Emerald went trotting up to the sisters and revealed what she knew, at this stage of the game, then he was under no illusions that his blood ties would save the relationship. There was no sentiment where Margaret was concerned about family ties, only a hard, cold suspicion. You were better off *not* to be related. His behaviour had been deceptive at the very least, even he couldn't deny that. It would now be in vain to state that he had only done it because he knew how unwelcome distant members of the family had been made to feel in the past. The door would slam in his face, and there would be an end of it.

Graham paced his small room, thinking desperately. Should he go back down there and ask her to maintain her silence long enough for him to discover what he had come to find out? Surely, she had no reason to want to protect her cousins... they'd treated her very badly. He was still deliberating on a plan of action, when there was a knock on his door. Scooping up the chart, he thrust it back into his briefcase, and put it once more under the bed.

On answering the summons he found Joan Evans in his doorway. There was no tray in hand this time, and she had changed into a revealing top, and a very short, tight skirt.

'Sorry to bother you, Mister Blood. I didn't get a chance to tidy your room up earlier, I wondered if you'd like me to look at it now.'

Graham stood back and let her enter.

'I'm just about to have a shower and go out, Mrs. Evans. If you want to tidy up, by all means, go ahead. I'll just get out of your way.'

'Oh, there's no need for that, Mister Blood,' Joan said, closing the door behind her. 'Barry's gone off in the truck to pick up some groceries for us, and for the shop. He'll be gone for about three or four hours. No hurry!'

Graham looked at her strangely. Any other time he would have been red-blooded enough to take her up on the offer, but just at this moment it was an unexpected development that he really didn't need.

Joan wandered over to the bed, and sat gingerly on the edge of it. Then she bounced on the springs a couple of times, her skirt riding up along her thighs.

'Isn't it funny? I'd never tried this bed before,' she said, coquettishly. 'You'd think I would have tried all the beds by now, wouldn't you?' She leant back on her elbows, and revealed a length of thigh that almost got the better of him. He shook his head slightly, then looked away.

'Like I said, I need to have a shower,' he said, excusing himself. He grabbed a towel and walked through the adjoining door into the en suite. Then he shut the door behind him, and she heard the sound of running water.

Smiling to herself, Joan got off the bed and began to strip. Once she was totally naked, she went over to the mirror and tied a small black band around her neck, with a tiny bow at the front.

'There you are,' she giggled. 'Gift wrapped for your pleasure, sir.'

She composed herself back on the bed, and lay in such a manner as to display all her charms as he re-entered the room. He certainly wouldn't be able to refuse this!

She lay awhile, listening to the sounds of him showering, and heard the water turned off. Then he was a while drying himself off, and she felt a prickle of anticipated pleasure run along her spine as she heard his hand on the door handle.

He pushed the door open and took two steps into the room, then stood there in his amazement, and his towel, staring at her lying on his bed. He had calculated that a rebuff such as he had given would have sent her scurrying for cover. Obviously he was wrong!

He had only been standing there for twenty seconds when the outer door suddenly swung open, and his eyes spun across to see who the unwelcome visitor was. Joan let out a yelp of terror, and struggled to sit up. It was Barry Evans, and he was fuming, to say the least.

'So this is what you get up to when my back is turned,' he yelled at Joan. 'You slut of a woman! Get out of here this minute, or I won't guarantee your life.'

Joan leapt of the bed and made a dive for her clothes, but Evans intercepted her and pulled her across towards the door.

'If it's all right to show it all off to a total stranger, then you won't mind running through the front bar like that to get back to your room,' he bellowed, and sent her spinning along the passageway outside with only her little neckband to hide behind.

He disappeared for a few minutes in her wake, and Graham listened with horror as he hurried her down the stairs. The door to the bar swung open and Joan was sent naked and shrieking through the room, to the great delight of a shearer, the mechanic from next door, and two prospectors who hadn't seen a woman for six months. Then Evans returned.

Graham was still standing, wrapped in his towel. He would have to tough this out.

'And you, Mister Blood! You can quit my hotel any time you like as long as it's in the next five minutes, and if I see you still hanging around in Heaven's Ridge after tomorrow, I've got a bull whip that I'll take great pleasure in laying across your hide.'

'Now hang on a minute, Evans. This wasn't my doing…' he began to expostulate.

Evans wasn't listening.

'Don't make matters any worse than they are,' he said, scooping up his wife's clothes. 'To stay under a man's roof, partake of his hospitality and then seduce his wife is not my idea of a friendly gesture,' he yelled. 'You're on a hiding to none, so you'd better make up your mind what it's going to be. Five minutes!' he snapped, then withdrew.

Graham cursed under his breath, and threw his clothes on in double-quick time. Then he gathered his belongings, and in less than five minutes was out in the street with a suitcase, a briefcase, and a bundle of dirty washing under his arm. He could hear Barry Evans' voice going full tilt somewhere at the back of the building, and Joan screamed three times before he wandered out of earshot, along the road. Luckily the service bay was never locked, so he went in there and dumped his stuff in the boot of his car. He could sort it out tomorrow.

Out in the street once more, he looked at his watch. It was only ten to seven, far too early to show up at Heaven's Ridge. They had invited him to 'dinner at eight sharp,' and he knew exactly what that meant in Margaret's rigid philosophy. *'Eight is eight, not ten minutes to or five minutes past,'* he imagined her snapping at him if he should be too early or late. He would have to kill time somehow. The worst of it was that he couldn't even go and have a drink!

Graham shot a look at the little cottage over the road. The curtains were pulled, and the light was on in what he took to be the lounge. He had a good mind to go over there and tear strips off Emerald Schuman, just for the hell of it.

As he stood there, undecided, the curtains wavered and a gleam of light lit up Emerald, peering through the curtain out into the street. She spotted him straight away, and disappeared for a moment. Then her front door opened, and she walked out onto the step. For a good two minutes they stood on opposite sides of the road, looking at each other, but neither made a welcoming sign. Emerald just folded her hands in front of her, and stared. Graham was the first one to fold. He wandered over the road, walked up to the little gate, and she beckoned him to open it and come in. He did so, without a word.

Passing through the front door he found himself in a chintzy little lounge room with comfortable armchairs, a large rug and a couple of scatter tables arranged round the room. There was no television set here, either, though there was a large wooden table by the window that was piled with papers of one sort or another. That was obviously where Emerald dealt with her paperwork. Interestingly, on the far end of the table was a modern computer with printer and scanner, all set up for the internet. The old girl wasn't as silly as she looked.

Emerald motioned him to sit down in one of the armchairs, one that had been barely used, going by its condition. Her own chair was a little more battered looking, and they both sported antimacassars on the arms and backs. They sat and looked at each other. Emerald was the first to break the silence.

'I was hoping you'd come over. I realize it must have been a bit of a shock to you this afternoon, and I suppose I shouldn't have sprung it on you so suddenly. But I'm so used to going up to my cousins and being kept standing on the doorstep, that the only way I can impart information is to gabble it out before they slam the door in my face. I suppose I've got used to that, now. That's one of the drawbacks of not having someone to talk to in a civilised manner. One forgets, you know!'

Graham stirred himself.

'Is it really so desperately lonely out here,' he said. 'Why one earth do you stay? Wouldn't you be better off back in the city?'

'Once a country girl, always a country girl, Mister Blood. Besides which, it's so very expensive these days. For a middle-aged spinster, with no work history and no job skills, life in the big city isn't really practical. Even life in little old Moonta, if you don't own property, can be very trying. I was left this place when my mother died. It's so out of the way that it's quite unsaleable, so it's not as if I could finance a home in Moonta by selling this. I decided that, given the freehold, it doesn't really matter where you live. Once that front door shuts on the world, you might as well live on Mars.'

Graham smiled, and began to soften up. She cleared her throat, and continued.

'Anyway, as you can see, I have the internet connected here, and that opens up the whole world to me. I can switch on and be in South Africa or China, or the Seychelles or England all in minutes. The world really is a global village these days, and in the future there will be so much information on the net that libraries will be things of the past. You'll just be able to download the book you want for a few dollars – in fact, I believe there are some sites where you already can. But the really great thing is the ease of access to genealogical records. That's my field, of course. Family history! *Our* family history.'

'So we have a common great-great-grandfather in old Theodore Schuman,' Graham said, musingly.

'That's right,' said Emerald. 'Or in your case three 'greats', because you're a generation further along than me.'

'Yes, I suppose that's true,' he mused. 'I don't profess to be any sort of an expert on the subject. I only know what my grandmother told me. She died two years ago. My mother didn't know much more. She died last year, and it seemed appropriate at that point to go in search of my ancestry for some reason. Maybe that's part of the grief process. Looking for something you've lost!'

Emerald nodded in understanding.

'I know exactly what you mean. There's something clannish about us all, when you get down to it... strangely enough, more highly developed among those of us who have no descendants, no family ties at all.'

'Well, that's certainly true in my case. My father died when I was seven of some lung disease he got working down the mines. His father before him died in a mining accident at Kalgoorlie, in 1958. That was long before I was born. So I've got nobody, really.'

'You're not married then,' Emerald queried, a twinkle in her eye. 'I *thought* you looked the part of the gay bachelor.'

'No, I'm not married,' Graham admitted, with an amused smile. 'Why?'

'Probably better that you don't pass the bad blood on. This family's had its day! Better that it dies out, now.'

Graham sat up at this, and looked puzzled.

'I wondered about that, when you said it the first time. What bad blood? My grandmother never said anything about that.'

Emerald mused silently for a moment.

'It all started with Ethel Williams, Theodore's wife. She was a barmaid you know, in Melbourne. You know what barmaids are! I understand she was a bit on the bawdy side, knees up on the bar, that sort of thing at the time that Port Philip Bay was full of ships bringing diggers to the goldfields of Ballarat and Bendigo. There were some pretty unsavoury types flooding Melbourne in those days. A lot of sailors deserted for the diggings. Anyway, I don't know if it was at that time, or just after they got married in 1865 – she was twenty-seven then – that she caught a good dose of syphilis. There was an old story that on one of Theodore's trips away from the diggings, he left a mate to look after her, and the mate did more than he was supposed to do in that regard. She certainly passed incipient syphilis on to her two sons, and I'm fairly sure that it developed during their lifetimes until it finally drove them mad. Gunther's wife was drowned in her bath in 1899, and even at the time there were some suspicions. Mind you, he went on to live another thirty years, but he was definitely loopy for the last ten years of his life. Frederick was dead by the age of thirty, but he was supposed to have been murdered by his wife. I believe she stirred copper sulphate crystals into his beer. No one ever found out why. She hanged herself at Moonta three days later. I have an idea he may have passed syphilis on to her, and she must have thought he'd been playing around. But he was born with it, nothing surer!'

Graham sat and shook his head in shock.

'I thought I knew a bit about the family, but I've never heard anything like this,' he said, incredulously.

'There's a lot more, don't worry. This family teems with tragedy. That's what I say, better it dies out now than goes on perpetuating bad blood.'

'Do you know anything specific about my grandmother? Why she left home! She'd never talk specifically about herself, not about that part, anyway. It was a bit of a mystery to me. It seems she took off to Kalgoorlie when she was very young, and never ever came back to Heaven's Ridge.'

Emerald laughed.

'Oh, that's way down the track. It all revolves around that 'punishment' room they've got up at the old house. There's a cell in there with steel bars... did you know that? Ethel Williams spent the last twelve months of her life locked up in it, frothing at the mouth. So they say, anyway. She died in 1874, after her whole face had turned black. True! She certainly paid a heavy penalty for the follies of youth.'

Graham looked reluctantly at his watch.

'Look, I'm going to have to put this on hold for a while. I'm due up at the house for dinner in exactly eleven minutes time, and you know what Margaret's like. She's a stickler for punctuality.'

'I know exactly what Margaret's like,' said Emerald, getting to her feet. 'Still, there's no hurry. I'm not going anywhere.'

'There's one thing I wanted to ask you.' Graham paused and pulled a wry face.

'I know... don't tell them that you're one of us! Now that I've met you at last, I'll say nothing else! I must admit, I did warn them off you this morning, but that will probably operate in your favour, knowing Margaret. She hates me, and would go against any recommendation I made, just for the hell of it.'

'Thanks,' said Graham, shaking her hand as he went out the door. Then he was out into the road and running before she even had the chance to say goodnight.

Chapter Eight

After his initial spurt of speed, Graham settled down to a swift walk up the hill to Heaven's Ridge, and kept checking his watch as he made his way along the driveway. He moderated his pace so he would arrive at the correct moment. He stepped onto the front verandah at exactly half a minute to eight, and the door opened fifteen seconds later. Margaret stood behind the door, smiling for once.

'Good to see you managed to make it on time, Mister Blood,' she said, standing back to allow him entry. 'We wouldn't want the food to go cold.'

She led him along to the foyer beyond the passage door, turned left and ushered him into the small, informal dining room, which was connected to the kitchen via a servery. Jane was already seated at the table, and Graham was ushered to the head of the table where he was to be the guest of honour. Margaret took the seat at the other end, and Ingrid was to sit on his left, opposite Jane. Ingrid was still clattering plates around in the kitchen, and it was some minutes before the first of the food began to appear through the servery.

'Good to see you could make it, Mister Blood,' said Jane, with a sardonic glance. 'We don't often have visitors, do we Margaret? Would you like to pour the wine?'

Graham noted the Riesling in the centre of the table, stood up and filled everyone's glass. Jane didn't wait, but quaffed half the glass in one mouthful. Margaret shot her a disapproving glance.

'Don't get carried away, Jane dear. Too much alcohol is not good for young ladies.'

Jane laughed, a most irreverent laugh.

'I hardly think Mister Blood would think of me as a lady. I'm far too earthy for that... wouldn't you agree, Mister Blood?'

Graham looked a little out of countenance, and stared hard at Margaret before he made his reply. She was sitting with her lips pursed tightly together, her hands clasped in front of her on the table.

'I'm not a very good judge of those sorts of things,' he replied, diplomatically. 'Perhaps when I get to know you better, you can ask me again.'

Jane laughed and clapped her hands.

'Oh, bravo! Well fielded, Sir. Was that at silly-mid-off, or silly-mid-on? I can never remember these things… silly of me, I suppose.'

Graham grinned, despite himself. She was a minx!

'I hope we're not going to have one of those evenings,' said Margaret, warningly. To Graham she remarked, 'Jane has a habit of lapsing into hysterics when she is over-stimulated, Mister Blood. We have to try and keep proceedings as calm as possible, so we don't cause her nervous system to be overloaded. Her mother was, unfortunately, the same… poor girl! It was an excess of *'feeling'*, an emotional instability that got the poor girl into trouble in the first place.'

Jane stared at Margaret in thinly disguised contempt.

'It was an excess of *'legs open and come and get it'* don't you think, aunt? Emotion had nothing to do with it. The only *'feeling'*…'

'Yes, yes, let's not go into all that, Jane, if you really don't mind.' Graham was surprised to see Margaret blush slightly. Jane's dart had hit home!

Ingrid showed her face at the servery and began to push plates and dishes of food through the opening, while Margaret lifted them off and filled up the table. There was a palpable silence while this was going on. Jane looked sullenly in front of her, and bit her lip. She seemed to be deep in thought about something. Margaret tried to avoid looking at anyone, but concentrated on arranging the dishes in some sort of order. Once that was done, Ingrid left the kitchen and walked around, smiling at Graham as she entered and took her place at the table.

Graham raised one eyebrow when he saw her. She was wearing a black gown, but different to the one he'd seen her in earlier. This was more revealing, and was obviously a far more expensive model. It revealed Ingrid's shoulders and neck, and she wore her hair down, just shoulder length, and pinned with a gold comb. On closer inspection, she had even applied a faint lipstick, and some eye make-up, all rather subtle, but enough to transform a middle aged spinster into an attractive, mature woman.

'You look very nice tonight, Ingrid,' Graham said, appreciatively.

Ingrid blushed slightly, and stared down at her plate. Margaret flashed Graham a glance, then looked at Jane.

'Oh, that's nice! Don't we look *'very nice'* too, Mister Blood?' said Jane, petulantly.

Graham cleared his throat, realizing his *faux pas*.

'Of course you do, you all do! But I just thought…'

'Don't embarrass Mister Blood, Jane! It's difficult enough for him, being outnumbered three to one,' said Margaret. 'Just help yourselves everybody. I see Ingrid has carved the roast, so we might as well eat.'

A few minutes passed where the activity consisted of passing dishes from one to the other, and heaping plates with roast potatoes, roast carrots and pumpkin and green beans, not to mention the beef. It was a repast fit for a king.

'Isn't this lovely,' said Ingrid, smiling happily at the faces around her. 'It's like a party, isn't it. A bit like the old days, when mother would invite friends over and there wasn't enough room at the table for everyone. Margaret and I often had to balance ours on our laps, didn't we Margaret?'

'That was a long time ago, Ingrid,' said Margaret. 'I'm sure it didn't happen too often… not from my recollections, anyway.'

'You never remember the good things,' said Ingrid, sharply. 'There were lots of good things happening when we were young. You've just blocked them out.'

'Perhaps the bad things outweighed them,' said Jane, between mouthfuls. 'It's like that sometimes… like my foot! After that happened, I felt that life was a bit of a swindle. It gave with one hand, and took away a foot.'

Ingrid looked at Graham, and waved her fork as she spoke.

'What do you think, Mister Blood? Is life a bit of a swindle? From a young man's point of view… you've been out there, in the world. What do you think of it all?'

Graham sat back and thought for a moment.

'You know… I think you get back what you put into it. Nobody gets a free ride anymore! We all have to work for what we get, and if that doesn't come up to expectations, then we just have to go out and work a bit harder.'

Jane finished off her wine, and reached for the bottle.

'Well that's not necessarily the case. I mean, look at us. We're still living off the plunder of a man that died a hundred and twenty years ago.'

'Jane!' said Margaret, warningly. 'We never discuss finances, you know that! I'm sure Mister Blood doesn't want to hear all about our financial arrangements.'

'Why on earth not, Aunt Margaret? Everyone's interested in money, especially other people's.' Jane suppressed a giggle. 'I know I am! I'm just dying to find out how Mister Blood makes his living. For all we know he might be fabulously wealthy, in which case he can come riding in here in his white Ferrari and carry me off to his twenty seven room mansion, and shower me with credit cards. I'm easy!'

'Jane! You horrify me sometimes! A moral, god-fearing woman would never sell herself for filthy lucre. Some things are sacred!'

'Ladies,' said Graham, shaking his head and laughing. 'Ladies! I can assure you that the only Ferrari I'm ever likely to own is the one my father bought me on my fifth birthday. It was a Dinky toy! I don't even know what happened to it now. I think a certain Michael Spinks pinched it one day when we were playing in the sandpit.'

'So you're not fabulously wealthy, young man,' said Ingrid, smiling and sipping at her drink. 'How disappointing! Now Jane will have to advertise.'

'Fat chance,' said Jane, pulling a face.

'Anyway... I'm not quite as poor as a church mouse, but perhaps a church cat might cover it,' said Graham, grinning. 'After this car repair of mine, I might just have to call in the receivers.'

'How's that going,' said Margaret.

'Another three days, the man says. So it looks like I might have to stick around, like it or not.'

'Isn't that rather expensive, over at the hotel?' Margaret asked.

'Fifty dollars a day. Not cheap if you're on a budget,' said Graham.

'What do you think, Ingrid,' said Margaret, giving Ingrid a pointed look. 'I think we should offer to put Mister Blood up here for a few days. We have the guest room after all, and it would be handy to have him on the premises. He is working here, after all.'

Ingrid scowled at her sister, and grimaced. The way they were sitting, when she turned her face to look directly at Margaret, Graham could only see the back of her head.

'I don't know. I think Mister Blood would prefer to maintain his independence. It's quite handy for him over at the hotel, and it's no hardship to walk up the road once or twice a day.' She flashed Margaret a false, brittle smile, as if to say *'get around that!'* '

Margaret clenched her knife and fork so hard that her fingers went white.

'We'll ask Mister Blood what he thinks, Ingrid. I'm sure you're wrong.'

Graham waved his hand, as if in embarrassment.

'I'd hate to put you good people out,' he said.

'Nonsense!' said Jane. 'It could be exciting around here with a man on the premises. I could lie awake at night and listen for the patter of little footsteps in the night, creeping from one room to another. We could have a contest to see who could get into Mister Blood's bed first.'

Jane flashed a brilliant smile at the other two, who looked totally discomfited.

'I really wonder about you sometimes,' snapped Margaret, angrily. 'You're making Mister Blood feel very uncomfortable. I can assure you, Mister Blood, she's only joking. Jane has this weird sense of humour. She thinks everyone else shares it, but she has to learn that it's most inappropriate... *most* inappropriate!' Margaret fell silent for a moment, then repeated, 'well, the offer stands!'

Graham laughed, and pretended to give in gracefully.

'All right! If you insist! I'd be honoured to stay in your guest room. As you say, it might save me a few shekels, and I certainly need to rein in the spending.'

'That's agreed then,' said Margaret, beaming for once. Ingrid put her head down and picked at her plate. Jane put her elbows on the table and cradled her face in her hands, then winked at Graham over the empty wine bottle.

'That's agreed then,' she mimicked. 'Everything's proceeding to schedule, I'm glad to see.' She flashed a knowing grin at Graham, which he took great pains to ignore. 'You should consider yourself highly honoured, Mister Blood. You're the first male to set foot in this house since old Mister Robert, who died in 1980.'

'She's talking about my... *our* father.' Margaret indicated Ingrid and herself. 'He had a heart attack, poor man, over dinner... just as we're here now. One minute he was perfectly fit and well, the next he collapsed over his plate and died. To me, that just serves to illustrate that when the lord calls, he doesn't stand on ceremony. Father hadn't finished his dessert.'

Graham thought for a moment, then something occurred to him.

'Is he buried around here? This seems such a long way away from the nearest town or cemetery. How did the family get on when someone died.'

Ingrid looked up and began to take an interest in the conversation.

'Did you notice the old wooden church down in the main street?'

Graham nodded.

'Well if you walk around behind the church, away from the road, you'll find all the relatives buried there. It's a bit hidden away because of the trees around the church, and the cemetery is some way back. But if you go for a walk over there you'll see all our antecedents laid out in two rows. Whenever there's a death, we open up the old church and pay a minister to come out and conduct the service.'

'It's usually closed up then, is it?'

'What? The old church? Yes! There's no call for a regular service here, not enough people,' said Margaret. 'Those that are here are base sinners, anyway. Far too worldly for us, Mister Blood! We rarely mix with the locals.'

'She means naughty sinners like Joan Evans, Mister Blood,' Jane whispered in a voice loud enough for everyone to hear. 'Are you sure she hasn't importuned you up to this point? It wouldn't be the first time that a casual passer-by has become entangled in Mrs. Evans' unmentionables,' she continued, grinning at the others.

'You really know how to portray the seedy side of life in the most visual of language,' said Ingrid, disapprovingly. 'Take no notice of her, Mister Blood. Jane takes a great delight in embarrassing people. The best way to deal with it is to ignore her. That way she'll give up in the end, and go off to her room to sulk.'

'Is that so, Ingrid? Well not this time,' said Jane, rather flushed now. 'No! I'm going to take Mister Blood on a tour of the house, so he can see all the ghoulish bits.'

'You are most certainly not, Jane!' Margaret's voice rang out. 'You can get that idea out of your head for a start. Besides, Mister Blood is not interested in our family's foibles, past, future or present,' Margaret declared, 'are you, Mister Blood?'

Graham demurred.

'I wouldn't say that, Margaret... sorry, *Miss* Margaret! I think your family is fascinating! There aren't many families that have managed to stick together they way you have, over a hundred years or more.'

'It's amazing, the welding power of cold hard cash,' said Jane, sardonically. 'Every generation has clung to the idea that they can find Theodore's missing fortune. No one has, of course. I think it's long gone. He probably got hit on the head for it in Africa.'

'Is that what you think, Jane?' said Margaret. 'I don't know where you got that idea. There was no question of foul play at all. He was involved in some sort of business deal with a man called Barnato. There was a fight going on between this Barnato and Cecil Rhodes for control of the diamond mines, with both of them trying to buy the other miners out so they could control the industry. This Barnato was a bit of a shady character. He used to buy up unproductive claims, which would then suddenly produce extraordinary quantities of diamonds. It was whispered that Barnato was buying up diamonds from other miners, from thieves and from smugglers, and salting these mines to legitimize his finds. But it could never be proven. I have an idea that Theodore got involved in buying up illicit diamonds for him while Barnato bought out every claim he could. The idea was that eventually they would share the ownership of the Kimberley Mine. In the meantime, however,

Theodore got sick, and died. There was nothing on paper, so Barnato would have ended up benefiting from Theodore's investment. Over three hundred thousand pounds. That's my theory, anyway.'

'What year was that?' said Graham.

'1883! He'd been over there some months at the time. The illness lasted only a few days, then he was gone. He'd expressed a wish in his dying moments for his body to be returned to his family, so they stuck it in a huge barrel of Port, and it sat on the docks at East London for weeks. When it finally arrived home, Gunther went down with a bullock dray to pick it up, and decided to leave his father in the wine so he wouldn't decompose during the long trip back to Heaven's Ridge. When he got here, two weeks later, he still wouldn't decant the body, so to speak, and it stayed in the wine for another two months. When they finally pulled him out, the body was as good as embalmed. Theodore was pickled.'

'Marinaded,' Graham commented, permitting himself a slight smile. 'Remarkable!'

Ingrid shivered in horror at the thought of it.

'Yuck! What a terrible way to go!'

'It served its purpose,' said Margaret, matter-of-factly. 'At least they got him home in one piece. It's a long way to South Africa, you know.'

'So you think the fortune was lost beyond redemption,' said Graham.

'No doubt about it! In my view, anyway. Of course, Emerald down the road has this idea in her head that she knows where the money's to be found, but I notice that she hasn't actually come up with any of it yet. I think it's a pipe dream.'

'Why don't you let her come up to the house, Aunt Margaret?' said Jane, curiously.

Margaret looked at Ingrid, and Ingrid flashed her a look that signaled caution.

'Well, it's not as if we grew up together. Their branch of the family, which is descended from Theodore's second son, Frederick, basically left Heaven's Ridge in the 1890's when Frederick went off to work in Burra, then in the copper mines at Moonta. They had their only son there, Lawrence, in 1897, and in 1900 Frederick's wife is supposed to have poisoned Frederick with copper sulphate crystals, dissolved in his beer. Then she committed suicide, hanged herself three days later. Young Lawrence was brought up by family friends of theirs. The next two generations

141

were born in Moonta, including Emerald herself. Her parents were left that cottage in the main street by Lawrence, I think, and moved back to it in the fifties. Emerald inherited from her mother in 1985, and moved up shortly after. She was a stranger to us. She came around, of course, trying to ingratiate herself with us, but as I tried to explain to her, Ingrid and I have always been sufficient to ourselves. We don't care for strangers, and we're certainly not going to welcome long lost family members into our little establishment here.'

'What Margaret's not saying is that Emerald seemed to think she had some sort of claim on this house,' said Ingrid, 'and we weren't going to open up our house to someone who was trying to take away our inheritance.'

Graham nodded sympathetically.

'Yes, I can see your point,' he said. 'I don't suppose I would have been too happy, either.'

Margaret got up and fetched another two bottles of Riesling from the kitchen cellar. They were cold, almost icy.

'Some more wine, Mister Blood? If you'd prefer spirits we have Jack Daniels, Jim Beam and Bundaberg Rum. Name your mixer.'

'The Riesling will be fine, thank you. I'm not in the mood for anything heavier tonight.'

'No, we wouldn't want to affect your prowess, would we,' said Jane, giggling to herself. She had obviously had enough already.

'What I meant was, I just feel mellow tonight. It's pleasant just sitting here chatting.' He shot a glance at Ingrid, and she had a little smile at the corner of her mouth.

'I was down at the hotel a little earlier,' she said. 'The most remarkable thing happened. I was standing just inside the door, looking around for Mister Evans, when suddenly Joan Evans came hurtling through the door from the stairway and across the floor of the bar, stark naked.'

There was a sharp intake of breath from Margaret, and a sudden squeal of laughter from Jane. Ingrid sat and waited for her to stop.

'Mister Evans was right behind her, shouting all sorts of derogatory things, including calling her a… dare I say it… a slut! She'd obviously been caught out, and Mister Evans was absolutely boiling with rage.'

'Is this true, Ingrid?' Margaret demanded. 'That's absolutely disgraceful! I knew the woman was loose, but I've never heard the like of that. Naked, you say!'

'As naked as when she was born,' said Ingrid, trying hard not to laugh. 'No... I lie! She was wearing something. A black ribbon with a tiny bow around her neck.'

This was too much for Jane who fell about all over the table, laughing.

'Good lord, I wish I'd been there,' she laughed.

'That's not the best of it. There were men in the bar, four of them I think. I saw their mouths drop open in shock, but they couldn't keep their eyes off her.'

'Typical men,' snorted Margaret. 'Any sort of salacious activity, and you will find them gathered around to watch. Present company excepted, of course,' she said, nodding towards Graham at the other end of the table.

Graham sat, quietly petrified. Why did these things always happen to him?

He cleared his throat as if to speak, but Ingrid turned towards him and looked him right in the eye.

'Would you like another drink, Mister Blood,' she said, meaningfully, fluttering her eyelashes at him. 'I'm sure it wouldn't hurt, just to have one more.'

'I think another drink would go down splendidly at this juncture,' he replied.

Margaret just sat and stared along the table, trying to imagine a woman running through the bar of a hotel, naked, in front of four men. The image was too much for her, and she excused herself for the night, asking Jane to make sure that she showed Mister Blood the guest room before she went to bed.

Chapter Nine

After Margaret disappeared, there was a difficult silence between the three remaining in the room. The old saying that two's company, three's a crowd seemed to fit on this occasion, as the two women glared at each other across the table. After a while, Ingrid got to her feet.

'I think I'd better clear away some of these dishes,' she said. 'They won't take care of themselves, unfortunately.'

Graham made to get up.

'Would you like me to give you a hand?' he said.

'I wouldn't think of it, Mister Blood. You just sit there and enjoy your drink. You're the guest of honour tonight. This is no hardship for me, I do it all the time.'

As she left the room, Jane pulled a face at her retreating back.

'That was a dig at me,' she said. 'I think she thinks I take advantage of the situation because of my gammy leg. I can't walk and carry dishes at the same time, you see, so she always gets to do it.'

'Do you think she resents it?'

'I think she resents *me*,' said Jane, pensively. 'She thinks that I've got it all, youth, good looks… the only thing she wouldn't swap with me is my footless leg.'

Graham stared at Jane thoughtfully, and had another drink.

'Don't you think you're imagining it,' he said. 'Sometimes, when people are thrust together in a close situation, various resentments arise for things that are perceived, but don't, in fact, exist! Have you ever spoken to her about it?'

'Of course not! We don't go in for philosophical discussions in this house. It would produce extreme doses of ennui, and there's enough of that already. Sometimes I don't even bother to get out of bed for days.'

'You need to engage yourself in some sort of stimulating activity, get rid of the cobwebs,' Graham said. 'I can't say *'go for a walk'* every day, obviously. But perhaps you should get yourself a hobby, something to get enthusiastic about.'

'Like collecting stamps?' said Jane, sarcastically.

'No, not collecting stamps!' Graham frowned! He found Jane's habitual cynicism difficult to cope with. 'No, I meant something a little more personal, something that gets the creative juices flowing.'

'Like making babies! Oh, yes please... when do we start?'

'I was thinking more of something like studying your family history, writing it down. After all, you have all the ingredients of a first rate read here.'

'Well, *they* made babies,' said Jane, mischievously, 'otherwise there wouldn't have been a history to start with. And hasn't it occurred to you yet that there would be no one to read this fabulous history of mine?' She poured herself another drink. 'Once Margaret, Ingrid and Emerald have gone, there'll only be little me, and I shall have flung myself off the cliff... Then there was none, she said!'

'What is all this rubbish about you flinging yourself off the cliff? Why on earth would you want to do that?'

'For exactly the opposite reason that my mother flung herself off,' said Jane, bitterly. 'She did it for shame, because she thought she'd been abandoned. She was overburdened with sin and guilt... thanks no doubt to her sister Margaret, and her uncompromising view of Christian morality.'

'I think you're being uncharitable there,' said Graham. 'I don't think Margaret would have been so unfeeling with her own sister…'

Jane laughed, a short hysterical peal. 'Is that right? Can't you see the way she's suppressed Ingrid, until she can't make a decision for herself anymore.'

'Did I hear my name being taken in vain?' said Ingrid, bustling back in through the door.

'Jane was just making a point,' Graham replied, hastily. The last thing he wanted was a confrontation between the two women.

Ingrid stole a quick look at Jane, who was studiously avoiding looking in her direction. Jane was beginning to look under the weather. She took another sip of wine.

'I was just telling Graham why my mother decided to take a short flight out of this place,' she mumbled.

Ingrid dropped a plate on the table, and in her confusion muttered an apology. She was obviously agitated.

'Your mother died in childbirth, Jane! You know that as well as everyone else.'

'Aaaah, poppycock!' Jane replied, staring into her glass.

'I think you've had enough. Don't let her have any more, Mister Blood,' Ingrid said, anxiously, removing the bottle and placing it at Graham's left hand.

'Worried that I might reveal too many family skeletons?' said Jane, goadingly. She looked at Ingrid in her most supercilious manner, and stared her down. Ingrid continued to pile the plates, and carried them around to the kitchen, shaking her head as she went.

'I think she might be right. You've had a few too many,' said Graham.

'Don't be a pillock,' Jane replied. 'If you want the truth, I'm the only one that's going to give it to you around here.'

Graham looked uncomfortable. He didn't want to provoke an argument, yet the vibes between the two women were becoming stronger at every exchange.

'Given that what you say is correct – about your mother, that is – what happened to your father?'

Jane slid around to face him directly, and pointed one finger directly in his face.

'You have a knack of hitting the nail right on the head... do you know that?' she said. 'Oh yes, my father! A happy chappy by all accounts... my mother thought so, anyway. Will Shire his name was, and he sold general hotel requirements. Glasses, coasters, towels, toilet paper, oh yes! That's how he met my mother. She was over at the hotel picking up something for her father, and there was this salesman there. Will Shire… Sweet William!' Jane burst into a peal of laughter. 'I don't know how they arranged it, of course. My mother must have been a rather accommodating sort of a lass – pretty well much as I would be, come to think of it… given half a chance!' She looked at him, meaningfully.

'Anyway! Somehow they managed to accomplish the deed over the next day or so, and he went merrily on his way, leaving his little box of tricks nestling comfortably inside my mother's womb. She had no idea! If she was as naïve as the rest of them around here, she probably thought she'd got away with it. It was only when her tummy began to move about that she realized she'd got a problem. By this time, Sweet William had made a few visits back to the hotel, more than was really required for the amount of disposables that little hotel was capable of going through. My mother met him there each time he returned, but once it became generally known that she was pregnant, she was locked in the punishment room every time he turned up. I've gleaned all this, by the way, from conversations that Margaret and Ingrid have had over the years. It took a lot of listening at doorways and feigning sleep to gather this information, I can tell you!'

'And what information is that,' said Ingrid, as she reappeared at the door.

She came back in and sat down, pouring herself another glass of wine. The worst of the mess was cleaned up. She thought she'd do the dishes in the morning.

'I'm just filling Graham in on what happened to my father,' Jane replied.

Ingrid choked on her drink, and took some moments to compose herself.

'Your father was an immoral man who took advantage of a young, naïve girl,' said Ingrid, forcefully. 'When the time came for him to live up to his responsibilities, he took off and never reappeared! And by the way, Jane, it's *Mister* Blood to you, not Graham.'

'I'm sure Graham is capable of telling me if my method of addressing him offends him,' Jane shot back.

Graham waved his hands at them both, in a gesture meant to calm the situation down.

'I never stand on ceremony, you know that, Ingrid. It's only your sister that perpetuates this *Mister/Miss* idea.'

'Unfortunately, if it continues when she's around, we'll all suffer the consequences,' said Ingrid. 'It's easier to go along with it.'

'Is that what you thought when your father locked my mother up,' Jane said, acidly. 'It was easier to go along with it! Didn't either of you come out on behalf of your sister, and fight for her rights? She did have rights, didn't she?'

Ingrid shook her head, as if dealing with a precocious child.

'It wasn't that straightforward, Jane. In answer to your question, no, your mother didn't have any rights, not in this house at any rate. Father ruled the roost! He kept both Margaret and I totally suppressed, as our mother did. She wasn't above locking us in the punishment room, well into our twenties. We didn't have the freedoms of other people. We thought it was natural for parents to have that sort of power over their offspring. I suppose you could say we were caught in a time warp.'

Jane thought that was hilarious!

'What do you mean, *'were!'* We still are, you crazy woman! Only this time it's your sister that wields the whip. I still get locked in my room, and I'm twenty five years old!'

Ingrid shrugged.

'I suppose that's the price we pay for staying here. You know where the door is, as I do. We choose to stay, therefore we choose to obey the rules of the house. The big sticking point is that our income is tied to the house. It's not portable! If we leave, we leave our income behind. There's a lot to be said for a comfortable income in this day and age, Jane. Isn't that right, Mister Blood?'

'Now don't drag me into it,' said Graham, distancing himself.

'Oh well,' said Ingrid, a little miffed, 'I would have thought that was self-evident.'

'Self-evident that a family can drive a poor young girl to despair and suicide because of *their* perceived morality!' said Jane, bitterly. 'I think it's disgusting!'

'I've already said, Jane,' said Ingrid, pointedly, 'that your mother died in childbirth! I should know, I was there!'

'Is that right, Ingrid?' said Graham, looking her in the eye.

She looked over at him, went to speak, then dropped her gaze. His was unflinching!

'There is always more to something than meets the eye, Graham. That doesn't mean that the story is necessarily wrong. These days they've identified a condition known as post-partem depression, and women have been known to commit suicide, or even kill their babies as a result.'

'That's still only a contributing factor,' Graham replied, his gaze fixed steadily on Ingrid's face.

'Oh, very well! Helen jumped over the cliff! Is that what you want to hear? We've covered it up for years because of the shame it would have brought on the family. If Margaret knows that I've admitted it to you, my life won't be worth living. So please keep it to yourselves!'

They both nodded in agreement, knowing what Margaret's temper was like.

'Don't worry, I won't say anything,' said Graham. 'And I'm sure Jane will hold her tongue… *won't you Jane?'* he said, forcefully.

'Yes master, anything you want, master,' Jane replied, with a mock salaam.

Ingrid looked quite upset.

'You can joke about it, Jane, but it's not your neck on the chopping block.'

'The truth might come out about my father one day, too.'

Jane looked directly at Ingrid when she said that, and Ingrid paled, and shrank back.

'Well, I wouldn't know anything about that. Margaret was six years older than me, and she tended to keep me out of things. It's possible that she went down and met Mister Shire, and told him to go away, that he wasn't wanted. That would have been after Helen was found to be pregnant. I do know that he kept coming back for a while, and was denied entry to the house. I suppose he just gave up in the end. There again, it might have been my father who did the heavy father act, and told him never to darken his door again. People did those sorts of things, even in the seventies.'

'I would have thought that a doting father would have insisted on a shotgun marriage. That was usually the way they did things,' said Graham, bemused.

'You don't know this family,' said Ingrid. 'We're different to everyone else. There was almost a perversity amongst the male members of this family to keep the womenfolk under lock and key. In fact, I had an aunt once, my father's sister, Elizabeth, who ran away from home for the very same reason. She got herself pregnant in the forties, and my grandfather locked her up in the punishment room for three months. I believe my grandmother took pity on her in the end, and let her out. She took off and never came back. I can remember my grandmother sitting in her old armchair and crying for hours about her lost daughter, when she was in her fifties. That must have been in the early eighties, because she died in 1984, having never seen her daughter again.'

'Well, I'd never heard about that one,' said Jane, indignantly. 'Maybe it's about time I sat down with you and Aunt Margaret, and got you to tell me all you know about the family. Maybe you were right, Graham. I do need a hobby! I think I'll take up family history.'

'If you're serious about that,' said Ingrid, 'perhaps you'd better go down and make peace with Emerald. I understand that she's done a full study of the subject, and knows all there is to know.'

Graham filled his own glass, then looked at Ingrid, got the nod, and filled hers. Jane was not impressed.

'Here, what about me? It's all right, I'm not drunk! It's been so long that the effect is starting to wear off.'

Graham looked at Ingrid, as if for permission.

'Oh, I suppose so. But the first sign that you're drunk, and it's off to bed young lady. I'm not sticking my neck out for you.'

'I must admit, this punishment room has got me fascinated,' said Graham. 'Everywhere I turn I hear it mentioned. How often was it used?'

'Go on, tell him,' said Jane, with a wicked grin. 'It's our own dark secret, isn't it, Ingrid? Where we all used to go to get punished.'

'Well, it all started off with Theodore's wife, I think. She went a bit crazy at the end of her life, and was known to have actually bitten people. She would fly into a rage and go for him with her nails, punching and kicking... I think the doctors of the time diagnosed it as GPI... General Paralysis of the Insane. He had a choice, either put her in an institution, or look after her here. He chose the latter, and built this iron cage inside one of the rooms. She was locked in there most of the time. During her few periods of lucidity she was allowed out, but they didn't last for long. Then back in there she would go.'

'Tell him about the little cage, Ingrid. The small one!'

'Oh look, I don't think...'

'No, go on, tell him! It's a revealing insight into the quirky nature of our male antecedents.'

'Now I wouldn't go so far as to say that,' Ingrid protested. 'That's just surmise on your part. You just made that up one day when you were being more than usually obnoxious.'

'I like that,' said Jane, laughing. 'I can remember you agreeing with me that it was the only explanation that fitted. Why else would it be designed that way?'

'Hey, hey you two. You've lost me! Just remember that I'm part of this conversation as well,' Graham laughed.

'This is hardly the sort of subject that is discussed between gentlemen and ladies, especially maiden ladies who are pure and virtuous,' said Ingrid, blushing.

'Even if they're only pure and virtuous due to the lack of opportunity to be anything else,' cracked Jane. 'Let's face it, Ingrid. The men were kinky! They must have been.'

'I don't really know what kinky means,' said Ingrid, and then burst out laughing in utter embarrassment. 'I know how silly that sounds, but it's true!'

'Forty-two, and never been kinked,' said Jane, cracking up, and falling about in her chair.

'Come on, Ingrid; Margaret's asleep by now. Let's show him the punishment room!'

Ingrid immediately panicked.

'No, no, we can't... what if Margaret wakes up? She'll kill us both!'

'Don't be such a softy. If we keep the noise down, she'll never hear us. She's at the other end of the house.'

Once Ingrid calmed her nerves, they crept quietly out of the dining room and tiptoed along the passage to the punishment room. It was directly across the hallway to the guest room, and was fitted with a Yale lock and a bolt. Quietly, Ingrid pulled a key out of her pocket, and opened the door. They all stepped inside, and Ingrid very gently shut the door behind them. The door was solid, and there were no windows, but once inside Graham realized they stood in a small entry area, blocked off from the room itself by another door, a heavy steel door this time. This was fitted with two draw bolts, heavy duty with padlocks ready to snap shut. Ingrid opened the second door, and they walked inside. Then she shut that door behind them, and turned on the light.

'It's all right now, you can make as much noise as you like. This room is totally soundproof. You can't hear a thing from outside the outer door, once both doors are closed. And you can't see the light under the door because of the inner door. That little entry point is unlit.'

'There's an observation window in the wall, through from that little entry area,' said Graham. 'Look, you can see through, into here, from the other side of the inner door.'

'That was just to make sure that the prisoner wasn't waiting to jump out on you as you entered,' said Jane. 'Like the one that went mad, I suppose.'

Graham looked around. The room was divided into half by a set of rusty iron railings, like a jail cell. Each bar must have been two inches thick. There was a door to match, with a fitting for a huge padlock, and inside this makeshift cell was a single bunk and a toilet in the corner. A small table was placed at the bottom of the bed, obviously for eating off. Otherwise there was nothing.

On the outside of the cell, there was an old armchair, somewhere for the jailer to sit and talk to the unfortunate behind bars. Over in the corner was a metal contraption about two feet high and four feet long, like a small cage. It was oddly shaped, with hinged doors at one end, and a narrow tunnel-like extension at the other. At the back end, in front of the tunnel, it had been left open.

'Got you wondering, has it,' said Jane, watching him intently.

'Don't Jane,' said Ingrid. 'You'll embarrass him... and me! We're not so brash as you are, nor so imaginative.'

'It's got me beat,' said Graham, mystified. It looked like a funnily shaped rabbit hutch.

'I tell you what. I'll show you how I think it was used, and you tell me if I'm right,' said Jane, giggling with glee.

'Oh, don't...' pleaded Ingrid. She put her hands up to her face as Jane hobbled over and dragged it out from the corner.

'I need one of you to hold this lid up,' she said, holding up the folding lid at one end. It had a half-round shape cut out of it, then a square box affair over the lot.

Graham held it up, and Jane maneuvered herself into a kneeling position in front of the opening, then backed herself into the cage. As she backed in, her legs fitted down and along the tunnel at the rear, and her body fitted almost exactly into the cage. Once in, her head was protruding, and she told Graham to lower the lid.

The half round section fitted over her neck, another hinged section came up from the floor to complete the circle, and encased her neck snugly in the opening, her head protruding. There were hasps in place to padlock these two sections into position, at which point the person inside would be well and truly imprisoned on her hands and knees. The box-like affair came down over her head, covering it completely, so that the only field of vision she had was the floor directly beneath her. It acted like a huge blinker, cutting off all vision to the front and sides. It was only when Graham stepped back to look at it from a distance, that it hit him. Jane's behind was thrust into the opening at the back, and totally exposed.

'Do you get the picture, Graham,' said Jane, wiggling her behind.

'Good God,' said Graham. 'I didn't even suspect…'

'Imagine the prisoner being thrust into this contraption naked,' said Jane, and I think you'll get the general idea.

'Say no more, Jane,' said Ingrid, still hiding her face. 'You don't have to draw pictures! Now, please get out of there… *please!*'

Graham held the hinged halter up and Jane managed to crawl out. He helped her into an upright position, and when she looked him directly in the face he noticed she was very flushed, and it wasn't from exertion.

'Get the idea, Graham,' she mouthed at him, then flicked her tongue along her upper lip.

Ingrid opened the inner door, and they all shuffled out as fast as they could go. Out in the passage, Graham pointed to the door of the guest room, and Ingrid nodded, and pushed the door open for him. He just nodded and watched as the other two made their way to bed, along the dark passageway.

Chapter Ten

When Margaret left the dinner table with the expressed purpose of retiring early, she walked swiftly along to her room, her cheeks burning. That vision of Joan Evans running naked through the bar of the Gold Ridge Hotel, in front of a male audience, had upset her no end. She entered her bedroom and shut the door firmly behind her, locking it with a key. It was a large room, with a single bed over against one wall, and a dressing table with mirror against another.

Once inside her room she began to pace, and as she did she muttered to herself, shaking her head as she did so. The carpet was well worn down the centre of the room, witness to the number of times she had paced up and down, back and forth across it, repeatedly, over the past forty odd years. Whenever she was agitated she would pace. Her head was so full of pictures that she dared not stop in case one overall vision rose up from these and engulfed her in some all-embracing sin that she would be unable to control.

'Slut!' she muttered, and twisted the beads of her necklace between thumb and forefinger as she did so. 'Slut! Slut! Slut!' She turned and paced, turned and paced.

Instead of calming her agitation, the act of pacing only seemed to make her more than usually nervous and out of control. Her lower lip trembled, and before many minutes were up she was visibly weeping.

'Get thee behind me, Satan,' she moaned, but visions of Joan's pink body, breasts, buttocks, soft flat stomach and her long naked legs loomed up in her mind, and ran in front of her eyes, ran and jiggled and displayed themselves while the men watching her bared their teeth and dripped saliva in anticipation of the ravishing of that body.

'Fornicator! Hussy! Oh, most fallen of women!'

She continued to pace, back and forth, but now caught a glimpse of herself in the dressing room mirror. Each time she passed it she was reflected back to herself, and it seemed to her as if there were two people pacing backwards and forwards in that room, pacing, pacing, weeping and struggling with the demons of carnal desire that had periodically risen up and possessed her body, searching for relief.

'Mother of fornicators,' she muttered, then gathered the neck of her dress together in a bunch, and bit on it in anguish. Still pacing she began to tear at her clothes, and rip them slowly away from her, the tears pouring down her cheeks.

'Why, mother, why?' she whimpered. 'Why do you ride so late, so late...'

And there was her mother, in the mirror, seated astride something that she couldn't see, and Margaret paced and paced, seeing her mother in the mirror each time she passed. She was bouncing up and down, as if she were in the saddle, and panting like a dog. She wore a fine chiffon top, blue, but it was so sheer that it hid nothing. She was naked from the waist down, her long, strong legs tensed and finely muscled for the task. As she rose each time her back arched and her breasts stood out, as if in intense pleasure, and there were fine beads of sweat on her upper lip.

'Mother!... Mother!... Hussy!... Slut!' Margaret whimpered, as she gave in to this indelible picture that had been etched on her brain twenty-five years before. Then, before she realized it, Margaret was standing in front of the mirror, naked, her poor body lacerated by the nails that she had clawed along her stomach and thighs, unknowingly, without feeling any pain, just an intense despair that rose up from some foul pit and possessed her very soul while her mother panted, panted, panted and rode endlessly through the night.

Suddenly the vision disappeared, and Margaret could see only herself in the mirror, blood running in rivulets down her stomach and legs, and the pain hit her, and she staggered at the intensity of it, then fell backwards onto the carpet in an intense swoon, and slept.

II

The following morning, Graham woke up and looked around, wondering where he was. He'd fallen asleep in his underwear, pulled the covers over him in the night, and now looked around the room, lost for a moment as to what had really happened the night before. His clothes were lying in a bunch on the floor, and he had a splitting headache.

'Oh, God!' he mumbled, as he rolled out of bed. 'Too much Riesling, that was what it was.' He looked around for his towel, then realized that his case containing his clothes and accessories were all down in the boot of his car, at the repair bay.

He looked at his watch. It was nine o'clock. He groaned.

He pulled his clothes on and, looking totally unkempt, poked his head out into the passageway to see if anyone was around. There were sounds of activity down in the kitchen, so he pulled the door behind him and wandered along to see who was up and about.

Ingrid was just finishing off the previous night's dishes and putting them away.

'Well, at long last,' she said, gaily. 'I thought you were going to sleep the day away.'

Graham sank into a kitchen chair, and groaned.

'I think I overdid the wine a bit last night… got a blinding headache!'

Ingrid laughed. She sounded as fresh as a daisy.

'No sympathy whatsoever, Mister Blood! It's called self-inflicted punishment. But I suppose I could make you a cup of coffee, if you think that would help.'

'It certainly would,' said Graham. He pushed his hair back out of his eyes and looked a little less like a scarecrow than before. 'I haven't got my stuff with me,' he said. 'I'll have to go down the road shortly and pick up my case.'

'Too late!' said Ingrid. 'I've already been down the road and spoken to Mister Giles. He opened the boot of your car for me and let me carry them back up for you. They're over in that corner.'

Graham looked around and saw his suitcase standing there, his briefcase next to it.

'I also took the liberty of packing your washing into a bag and bringing that back. It's presently in the copper, and will be ready by tonight.'

'You really are organized, aren't you,' he said.

'We have to be in this house, otherwise the chores wouldn't get done,' Ingrid smiled. 'We don't exactly possess the latest in appliances, as you can appreciate.'

Graham sat back in his chair and stared at her in fascination.

'Yes, I've noticed that. Why, if you don't mind me asking, are you determined to live as your great-great-grandfather lived, when there are so many aids for the home these days.'

Ingrid looked warily at the kitchen door, as if to determine whether anyone else was in earshot. Then she dropped her voice.

'It's not me, believe me! Margaret and I have had many a heated discussion about that very subject on many an occasion, but she is exceptionally rigid in her attitudes over things like that.'

'But surely you get a say! After all, you are basically half the establishment here.'

'Only the minor half, unfortunately,' Ingrid said, regretfully. 'I have no control over the spending, Margaret sees to all of that. She's a whiz with finance, much better than I would be... I'm afraid I would be a bit of a klutz.'

'Have you ever had the opportunity to handle money at all,' said Graham, sympathetically.

Ingrid carried the coffee over, and sat down, opposite him.

'I get a clothing allowance, and I buy through a catalogue. But I never actually see the money. Margaret pays everything by cheque, and she maintains a running balance for me, so I know how much I have to spend at any one time. It's all very theoretical to me!'

'Don't you see, that's a form of control,' said Graham. 'By ruling the finances the way that she does, she also rules you. Don't you resent that?'

Ingrid shrugged.

'It's never been any different! Since my mother died, back in 1984, it's always been the same. Before that it was either my father or my mother who doled out the money, and very little found its way into my hands. So I never really had the experience! I couldn't have coped with it if the responsibility had devolved on me.'

'Well, how did Margaret get her experience? It must have been the same for her, surely.'

Ingrid sipped her coffee, and looked up at him over the top of her cup.

'Well... no! She was always meddling in things when we were young. You can appreciate that she's always been a dominant personality around the house, even back when mother and father were alive. She and my mother clashed terribly, but Margaret would never give in to her. So in the end, she was given various responsibilities, just to shut her up, I believe.'

'Your mother can't have been very old when she died, if she died as far back as 1984.'

'No, she was only fifty-four. My father was fifty-four too, when he died, funnily enough. We're not a long-lived family. I don't think anyone has ever made it to seventy, not to my knowledge, anyway.'

'So what did she die of?'

Ingrid looked uncomfortable. She looked down into her coffee cup, then laughed, nervously.

'You have a way of asking the most awkward questions of people. No offence, but I've never really met anyone quite like you. You're so straightforward, so…'

'Personal?' said Graham, smiling.

'Well yes! But no, that's not really what I meant. You're so cold and clinical! Incisive! You say what you mean, ask direct questions without blinking an eye. You ask… I don't know, as if you have a *right* to know all these things, when other people just sit quietly and wonder about them in silence.'

'So you're saying that I'm not very diplomatic,' Graham chuckled. 'You're right! I've had that charge leveled at me on more than one occasion. My own mother used to say of me that if tact was a biscuit, I'd never open the tin.'

Ingrid laughed out loud.

'I like that! I've never heard that saying before.'

'No… it was one of her own. She used to make them up as she went along.'

'She sounds like a fascinating woman. Do you know, I know absolutely nothing about you, nothing at all! I know your name is Graham

Blood, that you can fix cupboard doors, replace hinges and paint swing sets, and that's all. I don't know where you come from, or where you were going to when I saw you in the bar of the hotel. I don't know anything about your background, parents, brothers and sisters, friends! I don't even know what you do for a living. Come to think of it, I don't even know whether or not you're married with five children, or have a permanent girlfriend or a doting mother.'

'In short, you don't know very much at all, do you,' laughed Graham.

Ingrid stared at him, at his blue eyes and straight, dark hair. She looked at the fine laugh lines at his eyes, and at his white, perfect teeth when he smiled. As she did so, she experienced a feeling of warmth and comfort. He generated a sense of security and well being that she had rarely felt during her life. She leaned forward, and stared directly into his eyes.

'Who the hell are you, Mister Graham Blood?'

Graham didn't get to answer that particular question, because at that moment Jane Wiltshire appeared in the doorway, hobbled painfully to the table and collapsed into a chair.

'Coffee and an aspirin, Ingrid... quickly, before my head explodes!'

'Not another one,' said Ingrid, getting up to revitalize the kettle. 'You're a good pair, you two!'

'Are you suffering too, Graham?' Jane said, looking blearily across the table. 'I don't even remember going to bed last night. Then I woke up at about four o'clock and tried to wander out, and my door was locked. Was that you, Ingrid?'

Ingrid looked around, and blustered.

'Oh, was it? I don't know how that happened. I was a little bit tipsy myself. Maybe I accidentally locked the door... I can't remember!'

'Hah!' said Jane, and laid her head on her hands. She didn't need to say anything more. Graham looked at Ingrid and raised one eyebrow, and she looked away.

'Where's the good Aunt Margaret this fine morning,' Jane mumbled into the tabletop.

'She went out early. I thought she'd be back by this, but she seems to be taking her time. She said she was going over to the hotel to sort out the new leasing arrangements.'

She turned to Graham.

'The lease runs out in about six weeks, so she has to decide whether she's going to offer to renew it, or put it on the market. I don't think she's too happy with the Evans's at the moment. That was a bit of a shock for her, last night.'

'You didn't have to tell her,' said Jane, looking up. 'If you hadn't said anything, she wouldn't have been any the wiser. I don't particularly like Joan Evans myself, but Barry's an old dear. It's not his fault if his wife's a slut!'

'We're all answerable for our actions, Jane! If you'd seen what I saw...'

'I would probably have stripped off myself and joined in,' Jane chuckled. 'Sounds like it would have been a gas!'

'You really shock me sometimes, Jane. I don't know where you get it from, certainly not me, nor your Aunt Margaret. Here, get this down you, and here's a couple of aspirin to fix your head.'

She put the coffee down on the table beside her, along with two tablets in foil. Graham got up and stood swaying on the spot for a moment.

'Well, ladies, I'm off to get a shower. I'll be out to paint the swings in an hour. If I don't make it, tell the paint brush to start without me.'

The two women watched his retreating back as he struggled out, carrying his two cases toward the guest room.

III

Margaret had woken up at five o'clock, still on the carpet. She was in pain, and took a few moments to get her head together. When she looked down and saw that she was naked, and noticed the dried blood, she began to whimper in horror. Throwing on a dressing gown, she checked that the coast was clear, then went to the shower and washed herself completely, feeling that she was washing away some congenital sin that had attached itself to her body. Then she smeared herself liberally with cream, where the scratches were the deepest, dressed and brushed her hair, and at seven o'clock left the house quietly and made her way along the driveway.

The pain she felt while walking she considered to be akin to a penance. It was like wearing a hair shirt, as the saints had done in medieval times. Scourging of the flesh! She thought of Luther, and of the pilgrims lashing themselves with leather thongs while painfully ascending the steps of St. Peters in Rome, on their knees. She felt righteous and clean, as if she'd taken on the devil and beaten him at his own game.

Barry was unloading the truck when she arrived at the hotel. The contretemps with Joan had only delayed his trip, not cancelled it. He had locked Joan in one of the rooms at the rear of the hotel before leaving for the second time, telling her through the keyhole that he just couldn't trust her on her own, anymore. She had screamed and protested, but he had been adamant. It was not the first time that Barry had caught his wife out.

Margaret walked up to him and, grim-faced, ordered him to meet her in the bar. Barry was under no illusions. His entire savings were tied up in the lease of this hotel, and he wasn't about to fall out with the owners.

'We need to talk, Mister Evans,' she said, when he bustled in behind her, looking rather shame-faced.

He had a good idea what it was all about. After Joan's rather ill conceived Lady Godiva act in the front bar, he had stumbled back through and discovered Ingrid standing there in the doorway, looking shocked.

'Look, I'm terribly sorry about that, Miss Ingrid. Terribly sorry! That woman will be the death of me, she really will. If only I could have married a good, faithful God-fearing woman, then I could have avoided all this. She suffers from a disease, Miss Ingrid… an illness. I hope you're not going to tell Miss Margaret about this.

You know what she's like, Miss Ingrid, she'll take it badly, very badly indeed.'

'I can't promise you anything, Mister Evans, I really can't! It was like the whore of Babylon tonight, running through the bar of *our* hotel. I believe I almost had a heart attack. It's in palpitation, even now. By the way, I need three bottles of Riesling, that Queen Adelaide one if you don't mind.'

'Anything, anything at all, Miss Ingrid. You only have to ask.'

'Well if you insist, a bottle of Jack Daniels, another of Jim Beam, and what's that... oh yes, Bundaberg Rum. Then I'll need some mixers.'

'I'll sort it out, Miss Ingrid, you'll see if I don't! I'll even deliver it, up on the front porch, in an hour Miss Ingrid.'

Ingrid had turned to leave, then turned back.

'Oh... and by the way. If you have a bottle of that Nut Brown Sherry...'

'Say no more, Miss Ingrid! It'll be my pleasure. And... you will be discreet, won't you, Miss Ingrid, I mean about tonight.'

Ingrid had smiled and left, but she had certainly not been discreet. Watching clandestinely from behind a eucalypt she had seen Graham erupt into the street with his cases, dump them in the car and then stand out in the road as if trying to work out what he was going to do. She had chuckled to herself, and made her way home, unseen.

'I've come to talk to you about the new lease, Mister Evans!'

Margaret stood stiffly with her back to the empty bar.

'Maybe if we go into my office,' he said, nervously. Joan was still locked in the room, and he didn't want anyone else wandering in at this hour of the morning, complicating things.

Margaret took his chair behind his desk, and kept him standing in front of her, at a loss at what to say. She was an expert at putting the opposition on the back foot, and dispossessing him in his own office was a good start.

'Now, about this lease! As you know, Mister Evans, it has always been the policy of my family to lease this hotel to people of good character. In fact, it is an essential condition of the lease that the manager and his family conduct themselves at all times with probity and integrity. They must show themselves to be morally superior to their clientele, and conduct their private affairs in such a manner that they are above reproach.'

Evans nodded furiously, trying to hide the fact that he was beginning to sweat profusely, and that it was running down his forehead.

'I know you understand all that, and I must say, in all my dealings with you, Mister Evans, I have never had occasion to take you to task over any aspect of your behaviour.'

Evans stopped nodding and began to smile.

'Well, that's very nice of you to say so, Miss Margaret. I've certainly tried to live my life in such a way as to reflect well on your family's interests.'

'However!' said Margaret, abruptly, brushing aside his self-congratulation. 'It has come to my attention that one side of the management, namely your wife Joan, has displayed herself in a less than worthy role in this very bar. I believe she was seen to be running naked… stark naked Mister Evans, in front of the patrons of the front bar, who were by all accounts leering and making coarse remarks about your wife's physical attributes.'

Barry wiped his forehead with the back of his hand.

'I can explain all that, Miss Margaret… it was a single instance only, a brainstorm if you like. She's not been well lately and…'

'Explain her bouncing her breasts in a man's face, Mister Evans? Explain her jiggling her naked buttocks dangerously close to a client's schooner, Mister Evans? I think not! She turned the front bar of the Gold Ridge Hotel into a house of ill repute, and the clientele of this hotel into leering, slobbering, lusting fornicators, Mister Evans. It's just too much, too much to bear!'

Barry Evans slumped into the seat usually reserved for the salesmen who were perpetually trying to sell him something.

'As a result, Mister Evans, I feel I have no choice but to offer the lease of the hotel to a different family, one that will uphold the morals and the values that I hold dear. I have been approached, as I'm sure you are aware, by two such families, both of whom would fit the criteria perfectly. So as much as it grieves me, Mister Evans...'

'But you can't, Miss Margaret. One little slip! And... *you know* what women are like, Miss Margaret. Present company excepted, of course, but a lot of women are over possessed by their... ummm... *sexual nature* if you understand me, Miss Margaret. They've never been taught self-control, and then they lose control of their feelings and... wham! Next thing they're peeling their clothes off in front of a total stranger. I know Joan's a bad girl, Miss Margaret, and what she did was wrong, but it would be very harsh on me if you took away the lease for something that I'm blameless for.'

'But there must be discipline, Mister Evans! Your Joan must learn that it is most inappropriate for a lady, especially for a married lady to carry on in such a reprehensible manner.'

'I agree, Miss Margaret, and I can assure you that I intend to take care of the discipline part of it as soon as you leave here. I have Joan safely under lock and key, at this very moment, and I have taken the liberty of obtaining this little leather strap to teach my wife the value of modesty and appropriate… errr…. appropriate behaviour!'

He produced a short leather whip made of knotted thongs, attached to a bound leather handle.

'Let me look at that,' Margaret demanded, her hand held out. He passed it over without a murmur. Margaret swished it through the air a couple of times, and whacked it onto the desktop. It made a satisfying crack. She handed it back.

'Spare the rod, and spoil the child, Mister Evans. I have always subscribed to that maxim. If that is the action you intend to take, then it may be possible that I might reconsider my position… but there again, I would have to be sure that such a punishment for her abandoned behaviour was actually carried out, you understand. I would have to be… present!' Margaret looked grimly at Evans, and waited for his reply.

'You mean…' he said, uncertainly, 'that you would want to watch?'

'It would be a possible way of redeeming your credibility, Evans. But I hardly think that is enough. One swallow does not make a summer, nor does one beating serve to reverse the behaviour of a most corrupt and immoral nature!'

Evans sat forward and grasped at straws.

'I'm in your hands, Miss Margaret. I suppose only a woman really knows what it takes to set another woman to rights. Do you have any suggestions?'

'Sometimes we have to be cruel to be kind, Evans. In this case, which is a very serious one of its kind, I hardly think that much can be effected in less than, say, a month! One month, maybe two! Given that period of time, I feel sure that by friendly persuasion and a liberal reading of the good book, especially of those sections that deal with the Jezebels of this world, the unholy whore of Babylon, along with a certain amount of, err, physical correction, I would be able to produce a change in your wife which would render her back to you as a faithful and modest woman. She would be chaste and worthy of you again.'

Barry sat back, and rubbed his jaw.

'A month? Four weeks? And you would review your attitude to the renewal of the lease...'

'Two months at most! And I could assure you, that if you delivered her into my hands – after this initial correction of course, which I think is only fair, and is your right to administer – then I can see no problem with the renewal of the lease in your name for, shall we say, another three years!'

'In that case, I think we should do it. I know Joan's not going to like it, not one bit, but she's going to have to learn. I feel confident that you will know the correct procedures to apply. My, err, only question is... do I get to see her during that two-month period. It's... aah... it's a long time for a man to be parted from his wife, if you know what I mean!'

Margaret looked at him and smiled.

'I take it that you are talking about your conjugal rights, Mister Evans. Don't be embarrassed! I am well aware of the type of lawful and wholesome intimacy that takes place between a man and his wife, in the blessed marital state. Of course you shall have access to her. Just give me two hours notice on any one day, and I will prepare her for your visit. You realize, however, that she may be resentful of you for a while, and may not be prepared to cooperate?'

'Yes, I had thought of that,' said Evans, slowly.

'You will be pleased to know that I have ways of presenting your wife in a manner in which she will have no say in the matter. You will be the complete master of the situation.'

'I don't know... she can be pretty fiery at times,' he said, uncertainly. 'When she gets in one of her moods, she usually fights me off.'

'She will be unable to refuse you, or to fight you off, I can assure you of that, Mister Evans! I possess an instrument of obedience at Heaven's Ridge that my family used for generations. Trust me! Your wife will be taught some of the greatest lessons of her life.'

'In that case,' said Evans, 'if you think it's appropriate, I think we'd better get this initial part over. She's down at the rear of the hotel.'

Evans slapped the whip on his hand, then led the way. Margaret followed sternly on behind, like an avenging angel from the Old Testament.

Chapter Eleven

Margaret returned home at ten o'clock with a spring in her step, and flushed cheeks, thinking herself to be an instrument of salvation for fallen women. She was glad that she had insisted that she be present at Joan Evans humiliation, as it was obvious that if she hadn't been there, Barry Evans would never have had the intestinal fortitude to go through with it. As it was Joan had fought and swore, and the devils in her body had arisen *en masse* to attempt to defeat the purpose of her instruction.

At first, Joan had circled warily around the bed, threatening to kill whichever of them came near her first. She even threw a couple of objects, one a vase, which shattered against the door. When she saw the whip that Barry held in his hand, she grew hysterical, and became even more so when Margaret fully entered the room from the safety of the doorway.

'What's she doing here,' she screamed. 'What do you think you're playing at, Barry? You're not going to touch me with that thing, so don't you get any ideas,' she yelled.

'I'm here to see that you submit to your lawful husband, and accept the punishment that he has deemed appropriate,' said Margaret, righteously. 'Your behaviour has labeled you a slut of the lowest order. If you seek redemption for your sins, you must submit.'

Joan looked at her as if she thought she'd gone loopy.

'Are you completely off your head? There's laws against this sort of thing, you know. I'll have the law on you!'

'There are higher laws than those of man,' said Margaret, sententiously. 'There are the supreme laws of moral behaviour that bind all women to be chaste in their actions and disciplined in the pursuit of their desires. You have shown yourself to be ignorant of these laws, or worse, contemptuous of their application in the regulation of your own life. Your behaviour has become licentious and perverted, and it is to bring you back to an acknowledgement of these precepts that we are here now. You *will* submit to be chastised, or risk eternal damnation at a later date!'

'Fuck you!' was Joan's response. 'Which asylum did you escape from, lady?'

'Joan!' Evans snapped. 'You've almost cost us the lease of the hotel! Miss Margaret has kindly consented to renew it, but only under certain conditions. If you don't comply, we're out on our ear!'

'If you think that's going to bloody well influence me, you're mistaken Barry Evans. I can't get out of this hell-hole quick enough!'

Margaret walked around the bed and fronted up to Joan as she backed against the wall. Joan put her hands out to protect herself, but Margaret seized her wrists, and Joan panicked the moment she realized how strong she was. Margaret's grip was like a vice.

She looked into Margaret's grim face, and found herself staring into a pair of eyes that reminded her of a snake. They were almost hypnotic! Joan felt herself being pulled inexorably out of the corner, and her resolve melted away. She went weak in the legs and began to whimper and plead to be spared.

'Don't hurt me,' she said. 'I won't do it ever again. I don't know what came over me,' she snivelled.

Margaret drew her out into the room, reached out and grabbed Joan by the hair. With incredible strength she then began to pull Joan's head down towards her so that Joan had no option but to bend at the waist. As her head was pushed further and further down, she suddenly gave up the struggle and began to cry. Margaret slotted Joan's head down between her knees, and held her fast, doubled right over. Barry stood on the other side of her, licking his lips, nervously. The Margaret looked at Barry, and leaned over her victim to pull Joan's skirt up at the back. Barry was presented with the clear target of his wife's buttocks.

'Now do your duty, husband!' said Margaret, sternly. 'And make it sting! Thus do all hussy's suffer the wrath of their rightful spouses.'

Barry had lashed out and scored his wife's buttocks with the thongs. She screamed at first, but then fell quiet as the stinging lash took her breath away, and sent her into shock. After seven lashes she fell to the floor, and Margaret looked down at her sternly.

'Please have her delivered up to the house within the hour. Two sets of clothes if you please, nothing fancy. We begin with lessons in humility.'

Evans had re-locked the door, leaving Joan sobbing on the carpet. Then he had escorted Margaret to the front door of the hotel.

'You may feel well justified in your actions, Mister Evans.' said Margaret. 'That exercise should have overcome some of the hurt you must have felt at your wife's salacious behaviour!'

'I feel remarkably good, considering the seriousness of the situation,' Evans reflected. 'I should have done that a long time ago. Thank you, Miss Margaret.'

'My pleasure,' said Margaret, tendering him her hand. 'Should you feel in need of any further release from your anguish, I will make your wife available for you to exercise your good right arm whenever you wish. It is important that she come out of this dark pit of illicit desire with a true knowledge of who her master is. Between us we will work the remedy, Mister Evans.'

With that, she sallied forth from the hotel, and marched up the road.

On her arrival at the house, Ingrid was still in the kitchen, but Jane had retired once more to bed. Graham was in the process of changing to go out the back, and paint the swing set, so Margaret found herself alone with her sister.

'What was the idea of locking Jane's door last night, Ingrid,' said Margaret, grimly.

'Locking her door?' said Ingrid, feigning innocence.

'Yes, Ingrid! I tried it this morning, at about four a.m. It was locked!'

'I'm sure I don't know what you're talking about!'

'Don't give me that, Ingrid. You're trying to sabotage my scheme, for some strange reason of your own. Don't you want Jane to get pregnant? What of the future of this family? We've talked about this on many an occasion, but now you seem to have taken up an opposite stance to me. Why?'

'Do I have to have a reason for everything, Margaret,' said Ingrid, sulking.

'In this case, yes, you do! I hope you're not nurturing the idea that Mister Blood is here for *your* benefit, Ingrid.'

'What exactly do you mean by that,' said Ingrid, blushing.

'You know exactly what I mean. You're letting your emotional nature take hold again, Ingrid. You must guard against such feelings! He's not for you! Mister Blood is a much younger man. You are forty-two, Ingrid, forty-two years old. He's, what? Thirty, thirty-one at most! There's a gulf between you, a veritable chasm of age. Twelve years, Ingrid!'

'I don't care, said Ingrid, suddenly. 'I don't care, and I don't think he cares, either, so there!' She bustled about the kitchen, wiping down surfaces in a flurry of confusion.

'Well, whether you like it or not, Mister Blood cannot have carnal relations with both of you, it's against God's laws. And as you are well past the age where you could bear children, Ingrid, Jane it has to be. That's only sensible!'

'I'm not interested in sensible,' Ingrid burst out. 'I'm sick of sensible! I've lived my life with sensible and it's time that sensible went on holiday.'

When she turned back to face her sister, there were tears in her eyes.

'I want to be loved, Margaret! I want to know what it's like to be held by a man, to be cherished and respected, and loved by a man. And I want to love him back! I desperately want to love him back, and show him that I'm not just a dried-up old spinster, waiting for the inevitable knell of doom to carry me off into a lonely grave. I haven't even lived yet. I'm forty-two, and all I've ever seen is Heaven's Ridge! Heaven's Ridge indeed,' she snorted, cynically. 'A fat lot of heaven we've seen in Heaven's Ridge. More like the Devil's Convent, Margaret, and we're the withered up old nuns waiting to be the Devil's handmaidens, and do his bidding.'

Margaret staggered back and slammed into the wall, as if she'd been slapped in the face.

'How dare you, Ingrid! How dare you invoke that name in this house? We have always been a god-fearing household and obeyed the strictures of the Christian Church. How could you possibly equate us with the… *'Devil's handmaidens'*. What a terrible thing to say. If I were you, I would be on my hands and knees, begging forgiveness for that evil thought, so that the lord doesn't send his angels down to blind you.'

'You're not me, Margaret! You're definitely not me! Is that what father made you do as a child, Margaret? Get down on your hands and knees, and beg forgiveness. I've often wondered about that! What did he do when he used to lock you in the punishment room, then go in there for an hour or more at a time, to see to your 'education', as he put it. I notice that our mother never went in there with him, Margaret. It was always you and him!'

'That's right! I got the punishment, Ingrid, always the punishment. You were the favourite but I was always having to beg forgiveness for one thing or another. And if you want to know, I

195

hated him for it! I hated them both. Our parents were sick, Ingrid, both of them, in their own ways. They suffered from a depletion of the spirit.'

'Is that why you poisoned him, Margaret?' said Ingrid, quietly. She looked her sister in the eyes, and saw the horror rising up to almost overwhelm her. Margaret began to gag, and ran hurriedly out of the room, heading for the bathroom.

'So now I know,' Ingrid muttered to herself. 'Now I know!'

II

By eleven thirty, Graham was out in the back garden, painting the swings, and Ingrid was hanging out the washing. Jane Wiltshire was sitting on the garden bench, and the three of them were engaged in desultory conversation. Margaret was nowhere to be seen!

When Barry Evans rolled up the drive in his blue truck, there was no one there to see him. Margaret, who had been setting up the punishment room, heard the rumble of the truck and came to the door. She watched as he coaxed Joan down out of the cab, and led her, chastened, up to the front verandah. She was wearing a plain cotton dress and a woollen cardigan. She'd obviously been crying, as her eyes were puffy and swollen.

She gave him some resistance when he tried to pull her over to the front door, but the moment Margaret stepped out, all resistance ceased. It was almost as if Margaret wielded some sort of mental power over her, Barry thought, because she seemed incapable of resisting Margaret's hypnotic stare. It was like a cobra playing with its prey.

Joan was ushered in through the front door, and marched swiftly along the passages to the punishment room. The doors were open, so she was marched straight in, and Barry was allowed to follow. It was the work of only moments to secure Joan behind the bars in the cell, and then Margaret turned back to Barry and said, 'what do you think?'

Barry was looking around, appraising the little room.

'Quite a little prison cell you've got here,' said Barry, appreciatively. 'I don't think she'll be giving *you* much trouble, Miss Margaret. You seem to have the situation well under control.'

He pulled the whip out from under his coat, and offered it to Margaret. She placed it conspicuously draped over the back of the armchair, facing the cell. It would give Joan something to think about.

Joan sat forlornly on the bed, the forgotten woman. Neither of them addressed themselves to her, she had become simply 'the problem'.

Barry looked over at the smaller cage that Jane had demonstrated so effectively to Graham and Ingrid the night before. He shook his head, musingly.

'Now that's the strangest looking contraption I've ever set eyes on. Would I be wrong in thinking that cage is for a grown-up person?'

'No, you're quite correct, Evans. That cage has been in use in this house for correctional purposes since 1872. I believe that's when my great great grandfather had it fashioned to restrain his wife, who through her libidinous behaviour had contracted that terrible instrument of God's wrath – syphilis! In the tertiary stages of that, she became totally deranged, and that was designed to prevent her from attacking him whenever he entered the room. It was very efficacious.'

'I see! Well, I'll leave her in your good hands, and get back to my work. All this kerfuffle has put me way behind.'

'I'll see you safely out, Mister Evans. You can relax now. The problem is in hand, and I can begin the program of reclamation.'

They went out and locked both doors, leaving Joan staring at the cage, and pondering her immediate fate.

Margaret saw Barry off, then went down to the rear of the house and out into the garden. Ingrid was still at the line, hanging out clothes, so she wandered over to her and stood, waiting for her to stop. She spoke quietly.

'I'm going to need that key, Ingrid, the one you took off the main keyring… the one for the punishment room.'

Ingrid looked at her in surprise.

'What on earth do you want that for? We don't use it any more.'

'I don't like sensitive keys floating loose around the house. I'll take it now, if that's all right with you. The room will be kept locked from now on, and as you know, it's out of bounds to our guest.' She nodded towards Graham, who appeared to be caught up in his work.

Ingrid took the key from the pocket of her dress and handed it over. There was no use arguing with Margaret over this, she would get her own way in the end. Margaret took it and dropped it into her own pocket. Then she walked over to Graham.

'I have another little job for you as soon as you've finished those swings. Come and see me inside when you're ready.'

'I have another little job for you,' mimicked Jane as Margaret disappeared into the house. 'You see that little girl with the peg-leg, well I want you to bend her over the...'

'Jane!' Ingrid remonstrated. 'I hope we're not going to have to put up with another gem from your over-active imagination! Leave Graham to get on with whatever it is he has to do, if you don't mind. He, unlike you, is here to work!'

Graham stood up straight and surveyed the finished swings. He stretched and massaged the small of his back.

'I think it's time we all took a coffee break, don't you, girls? Margaret's little job can wait a while. What say we all go for a walk down to the old church? I feel like a wander through the family crypt so to speak! How about showing me the graves of all these people you've been telling me about?'

'Do you think we should?' said Ingrid, uncertainly. 'Margaret might not be too impressed.'

'Oh, bugger Margaret, Ingrid,' Jane put in. 'You two go ahead. I'm not in the mood for hobbling all that way just for a bunch of old graves. I'll entertain myself while you're gone.'

'Very well, we'll cut around,' said Ingrid, leading him to the gate on the eastern side that Jane had entered, on that second day.

There was a narrow pathway leading down the hill towards the main street, and it came out opposite the old, wooden church. They only had to cross the road and walk around behind it, and Graham could see the cemetery laid out amongst the trees.

The first headstone in the left-hand row was that of Gunther Schuman, departed this life 29th September 1930. Next to him was Bernard Schuman, Gunther's only son, passed away in his sleep, 12th June 1959 at Heaven's Ridge. Buried in the same plot was Bernard's wife, Barbara Schuman, nee Bissell, who passed away 1st July 1966.

Ingrid and Graham wandered slowly along the line of headstones, sensing the sadness of this last resting place. Lawrence Schuman was next. He was descended from the other side of the family, from Theodore's second son, Frederick. He had died at Heaven's Ridge on the 13th December 1954, though there was no sign of his wife, Julia Goldsworthy. Graham turned to Ingrid and asked why.

'She outlived him by about fifteen years, and died in Burra. I think it was in the February, in 1969, but we were only informed about it second hand. I wasn't even a teenager at the time.'

Graham nodded, and kept walking.

There were two graves separated by some unused plots, further into the bush. The first was that of Emily Forster, wife of Gunther, who died in her bath, 4th April 1899. The headstone was badly weather-worn, and had not been tended. The other was that of the infamous Ethel Williams, quarantined from the rest of the cemetery by several yards. She died in a raving fit on 1st October 1874. The headstone didn't report this however, it just said *'Christ's fallen child, in his healing arms'*, and the date.

In the opposite row, working back towards the church, the first headstone reflected that

Theodore Schuman, of revered memory, had departed this life in Kimberley, South Africa on the 30th November 1883.

'Is he actually buried there,' said Graham. 'That's more of a memorial stone, the sort of thing one puts up when there's no body to bury.'

Ingrid shrugged and looked nonplussed.

'I rarely come over here. I wouldn't know about most of these,' she replied, evasively.

She came up and stood beside him, and stared down at the slab. Her shoulder was touching his arm, and they stood there silently for a while, meditating on the myth of the old prospector who had made good. Graham quietly reached down and grasped her hand in his, and she jumped a little. He squeezed her hand, and she blushed, and squeezed back. Then they looked quietly at each other, and looked away again. Graham squeezed her hand once more, then let it go, and Ingrid felt a shiver run through her frame, of excitement. She could feel her heart pounding in her chest, and the blood rush to her temples. Graham put his hand in the small of her back, and they moved on to the next grave.

Here lay Robert Schuman, Ingrid's father, and Graham noticed that she suddenly seemed overcome by some emotion, and turned away.

'Here lies Robert Schuman, departed suddenly 4th August 1980.'

Graham looked at Ingrid's back, then looked back at the headstone. It was covered in some sort of evil looking moss that had eaten into the face of the stone like some sort of plague. Perhaps that was what had upset Ingrid. The lichen was a blue-green, and seemed to have acidic properties because where it had died off it left behind pits and holes in the stone's face. This noxious weed had spread to the next headstone as well, and Ingrid refused to look at this altogether. It was that of her mother, Louisa Chapman. *'Faithful wife of Robert,'* the headstone read, *'died lamented 16th January 1984.'*

Ingrid turned and tugged at his sleeve.

'Let's go, I can't stand this place,' she said. 'Too many memories for me!'

Graham raised an eyebrow, and moved off, walking beside her. As they walked alongside the church, and fell in its shadow she suddenly clutched at his sleeve and spun him around to face her.

'Do you like me, Graham? I have to know!'

'What on earth? Of course I like you, Ingrid, I thought that would be self-evident.'

Ingrid stamped her foot, impatiently.

'You know what I mean! Do you *really* like me? I mean, *really!*'

'Yes, Ingrid! Yes! I *really* like you. What's all this about?'

Ingrid looked away, then spun in a circle and shook her head. She raised her hands to her face and shielded her eyes, as if trying to reword her question.

'Oh, it's no good... I suppose you *really* like everyone! You're just that sort of person.' She looked at him, questioning, but he just looked back at her, blankly.

'Is that it... you really like everyone?' She paused for a moment. 'I suppose you really like Jane, as well.'

Graham looked up in the air, as if deliberating.

'Jane....' he said, ruminatively. 'Yes, I must admit, I *do* like Jane. She amuses me!'

'You *do* like Jane... oh well, that's it then! I suppose Jane has so much going for her, doesn't she? Youth, good looks, a young body...'

'But only one foot,' Graham cut in. Ingrid looked at him, and saw he was laughing at her. She punched him on the arm.

'Don't you dare to laugh at me, Graham Blood! This is very difficult for me.'

'Is it? I thought you were doing very well, so far.'

'You're making fun of me. Oh, what am I doing? Look at me, a forty-two year old spinster making a fool of myself. Forget I ever said anything! I didn't say it!'

'Didn't say what,' said Graham, assuming a look of total innocence. 'If you didn't say it, how could I have heard anything?'

'You really are a beastly man at times, Graham Blood!'

Ingrid went to storm off, but Graham caught her by the arm and pulled her back into the shadows.

'I didn't say I *really* liked Jane, did I? I said I *do* like Jane... which is different!'

'How different?' Ingrid said, facing him now against the wall of the church.

As if in answer, Graham drew Ingrid towards him and put his hands on her waist. Then he leant towards her and waited for her to reciprocate. Their lips were very close together.

'If this is a tease, Graham Blood, then I'm going to be very angry with...'

The rest of the sentence was lost as he clamped his lips down on her mouth and kissed her. Ingrid gave herself up to that kiss, the first real kiss since that time down by the old shed with Johnny Morrison. After a second kiss that lasted for twenty seconds or more, Ingrid unaccountably burst into tears.

Chapter Twelve

While Graham and Ingrid were down at the church, Jane sat and read a magazine in the garden for a while, but then that became tedious so she returned to the house. As she limped along the passageway, Margaret suddenly appeared from the punishment room and without seeing Jane, turned and locked the door behind her. She was about to walk off up the passage when she heard Jane behind her and turned with a start.

'Oh, it's you, Jane! You gave me a fright! I thought you were all out in the garden.'

'No, I got fed up, so I thought I'd come in.'

'What's the matter... aren't the other two keeping you company?'

Jane looked at Margaret suspiciously. She looked unnaturally flushed for some reason, and seemed to be rather nervous. She flashed a look at the door of the punishment room, and then back at Margaret.

'They've gone for a walk to the old church.' She was silent for a moment, then said, 'is there anything I should know about?'

'Nothing that concerns you, Jane! But, come to think of it, I think it's time we had a little chat. Come through to the study.'

The study lay along the passageway forbidden to visitors. There were only two doors along that side, and the study was one of them. It was actually a study and a library, with walls of shelves filled with the most interesting of volumes. Jane had never had access to it, as Margaret kept it locked at all times.

When they entered, Margaret closed the door behind them, and motioned Jane to a comfortable chair. Jane looked about her in curiosity.

'So this is the mysterious study, where old Theodore counted his money. I can't see anything so terrible about this room, Margaret. You used to tell me that it wasn't a fit place for young ladies to go.'

'And so it isn't, Jane! There are certain volumes on these shelves, which, for want of a better term, would have rather a corrupting effect on a young, innocent woman. The older gentlemen in days gone by used to collect these volumes as curiosities. In those days they were considered to be enlightening. Today we would call them pornographic. The only reason I haven't destroyed them is that they happen to be worth a considerable amount of money, and I've never believed in throwing good money away.'

'Oh, goody! Something to while away the sleepless hours before dawn, while I lie masturbating in my narrow bed.' Jane looked at her aunt, guilelessly.

'I wish you wouldn't say things like that, Jane! You make me feel most uncomfortable when you come out with these disgusting little sayings of yours. Please have some respect for my feelings!'

'Sorry aunt,' Jane said, suppressing a grin, 'I keep forgetting that you don't masturbate.'

Margaret shook her head, and tried valiantly to ignore the last remark.

'What I've brought you here for, Jane, is to talk to you about Ingrid. I'm very worried about her. I think she's going through what some people might term a mid-life crisis.'

'I hadn't noticed anything of that nature,' said Jane, astonished. 'If anything I think she's been happier, lately, than I've seen her in ages.'

'That may be so, but from whence does that happiness spring? Ask yourself that!'

Jane shook her head, and looked blank.

'I'm afraid that Ingrid is falling for that young man, Mister Blood. She is of an overly romantic nature, always has been, though it's been well suppressed for years. On the few occasions that she's happened across personable young men in the past, which hasn't been very often, I've managed to steer her back to the straight and narrow without too much damage being done. This time, she's proving to be more intractable.'

Jane took this in, and then began to laugh.

'You can't be serious, Aunt Margaret! Ingrid... and Graham! Now that's just too hilarious for words. She's almost old enough to be his mother, for god's sake.'

'Barely, but given modem morals I suppose you're right. The fact is I can see she has her heart set on him, and she is developing expectations that are unrealistic in the extreme. She expects him to reciprocate, and of course, that is highly unlikely. However, if she continues to lavish attention on him, he - being a man - may very well seek to take advantage of her, even at her advanced age, and this could very well destroy her faith in human nature once and for all. If he happened to seduce her... No! Hear me out...'

She tried to continue as Jane collapsed laughing at Margaret's quaint phraseology.

'If he did, then decided to disappear... then I fear she might well try something stupid.'

Jane suddenly became serious.

'You mean she might try to kill herself? Surely not! She's too sensible for that.'

'There's no telling what might happen in affairs of the heart,' Margaret said, soulfully.

'Well what can I do about it? It's hardly up to me!'

'That's where you're wrong, Jane. You see I've seen him looking at you, watching you while your attention was engaged elsewhere. I think he's very taken with you, Jane. It would only need a little push from you, and he'd be dancing attention on you. That would show Ingrid how futile it was before it's too late. I really need your help in this, Jane!'

Jane looked into the middle distance, and bit her lip.

'I can't imagine what else I'd have to do! I've tried just about everything, bar waving my knickers in his face. I don't think he's interested in me at all.'

'You'd be surprised, my girl. The ways of young men are often an enigma to young women. It's hard to understand the male psyche! But you shall have my complete cooperation in anything you deem necessary to lure him away from Ingrid.'

'Including luring him to my bed,' said Jane, surprised at this about-face.

'I would even turn a blind eye to fornication, if that's what it takes to save my sister from herself,' said Margaret, self-righteously. 'Sometimes, the only way to defeat the devil is to use the devil's tools.'

'Well that's putting it rather bluntly. So I'm to be the sacrifice!'

'As long as it's done in a good cause, the lord will forgive you, Jane. Will you do it?'

'Of course I will, anything to oblige. I quite fancy the man, as a matter of fact... though I'd never admit as much to him, of course.'

'Of course,' nodded Margaret. 'I shall make sure that Ingrid doesn't get the opportunity to lock you in your room again. She only did it out of jealousy. Perhaps you could make your way to his room when everyone else is asleep. Then let nature take its course.'

'Sounds good to me, Aunt Margaret. And... hey! You're not such a bad old stick after all.'

II

Once Ingrid had recovered her composure, helped by a sympathetic hug from Graham, they headed back across the road, oblivious to anyone else but themselves. They weren't exactly a picture of young love, as Ingrid very properly insisted that they keep a decorous distance between them once they left the shadow of the old church. But to Barry Evans, who was outside the pub taking a breather, to see his wife's would-be seducer in the close company of the sister of the woman who was taking Joan in hand, was a severe shock to the system.

Barry hadn't really given any real thought as to where Graham would stay once he threw him out of his room in the hotel. What's more, he hadn't really cared! The very last thing he expected was that the young seducer would end up under the same roof as that of the seducee! The hairs on the back of his neck rose up in protest, and he almost forgot himself, and marched up the road to give the young man a piece of his mind. Then he remembered the lease! It wouldn't do to give way to emotional outbursts, especially as Ingrid had shown herself to be untrustworthy where it came to keeping secrets from her sister. Instead, he turned and stomped back into the front bar of the hotel, poured himself a schooner and downed it in one draught.

Then he glared at himself in the mirror behind the bar! The mirror gave him no relief from his black thoughts. All he could see reflected back was the figure of his naked wife lying spread-eagled on the bed, waiting to be ravished by a fee-paying guest. He downed a second drink, then stomped out of the bar once more, and into the street.

Ingrid and Graham had disappeared along the snaking track that led up the hill. Ten yards off the road, anyone taking that path was totally hidden by the eucalypts. He grunted in frustration, and then let his eye fall on Emerald Schuman who was doing a bit of spying on her own, under the guise of weeding her patch. He made his mind up, and strolled across the road.

'Good afternoon, Miss Emerald. Lovely day today!'

Emerald looked around and noticed him for the first time. She seemed surprised! Although she'd had many dealings with the hotel manager in the past, it was a rare occasion when he'd gone out of his way to cross the road to talk.

'Good afternoon, Mister Evans. It is a lovely day, isn't it!'

They eyed each other warily, each of them filled with question marks about the other. Barry knew that the sisters had no time for their cousin. He'd heard a hundred times how they'd slammed the door in Emerald's face, or had ignored her summons as they ambled past on the way to the hotel, their noses in the air. Emerald had heard about Joan's humiliation in the bar, and had been told later that 'that Blood fellow was naked in a room with her, and up to no good.' She knew where he had gone, but was keeping her own counsel in the matter, and was content to maintain a watching brief

'I need to talk to you, Miss Emerald. I'm in a bit of a quandary here, and to be honest I don't know what to do about it.' He looked guiltily up and down the street as if he was fearful of being overheard. Emerald got the message.

'If it's a private matter, Mister Evans, I would be delighted to ask you into my little parlour for a chat.'

'It is that, Miss Emerald, it is that! Rather embarrassing actually.'

They went inside, and Evans was ushered into the same chair Graham had occupied only the evening before.

'Now how can I help you, Mister Evans?'

'It's about my wife, Miss Emerald. I suppose you know about the problem that arose last night, when I had to come back unexpected like, to pick up a spare tyre?' Emerald nodded, in a disinterested matronly fashion. 'Well, I found her with that lecherous young fellow, stark naked she was, and he not much better with just a towel around him. It was like a scene from the Arabian Nights, or so I'm given to believe, not having actually read the Arabian Nights you understand.'

Emerald nodded again, and suppressed a smile.

'Anyway, I threw him out on his ear! Now, unless I'm much mistaken, he's staying up at Heaven's Ridge! Would you be able to confirm that... I mean, you usually seem to know what's what and who's who about the place.'

'I couldn't be certain of course, but I do know that he was invited to dine there last night. I believe he did keep the appointment! It wouldn't be too hard to guess that from there he was invited to stay the night... in the guest room, of course. There would be no impropriety under Margaret's roof, you can be sure of that.'

'No, no, I know Miss Margaret and her ways. She's strict, but fair I'd say. But...' Here Evans's frustration seemed to boil over. 'I've got to wondering just who the blazes he is, Miss Emerald. I mean, it's a little bit out of the way here, if you get my drift, and yet this young bloke arrives here and manages in a couple of days or so to finagle his way into the confidence of the sisters, who are known far and wide for their inhospitality. As you know only too well - and you're a cousin, Miss Emerald! They're not known for having guests to stay, or even visitors to visit! I can count the number of times I've been in that house on the fingers of one hand, Miss Emerald, and I've been here for donkey's years.'

'I sympathise, Mister Evans. I haven't managed to get beyond their doorstep once. They think the worst of me, for some strange reason of their own.'

'Yet this young Blood gets in there first pop! I think it's strange, Miss Emerald, very strange if you ask me.'

Emerald didn't often get the opportunity to talk to anyone, and for someone as naturally loquacious as her, bursting with information and with no one to confide it to, this was too much for her.

'Well, I do happen to have a bit of inside information as a matter of fact, but if I should let you in on it, you must swear that it remains in this room, between the two of us. I don't want to cause anyone any problems by being too loose-lipped.'

'You can rely on me, Miss Emerald. My lips are sealed,' Barry replied, his cars pricking up. 'I wouldn't divulge a confidence, not for... not for all the tea in China,' he said, solemnly.

Emerald leaned forward in her chair, and lowered her voice, conspiratorially.

'I believe Mister Blood's interest in the sisters and their affairs lies a lot deeper than water, Mister Evans.'

Emerald sat back, pleased at her conundrum. Barry looked baffled.

'Blood... water... Mister Evans? Blood and water!'

'You mean blood is thicker than water, Miss Emerald! I see!' said Evans, not seeing at all. 'So how...' He tailed off into silence.

'Mister Blood is of *the* blood! It just so happens that Mister Blood is my third cousin, once removed I believe is the saying. He's a generation further along than me.'

'He's your cousin! Well that must mean that he's their cousin as well! Well, well, well! There's one come out of the woodwork! Does Miss Margaret know this?' he asked, sharply.

Emerald shook her head, violently. She suddenly had a bad feeling about this.

'No, she most certainly does not! That's why I swore you to silence Mister Evans. If she finds out that he's related in any way, she will slam the door in his face, just as surely as she slammed it in mine.'

'Is that so,' said Evans, sitting back with the glow of revelation on his face.

'I must insist that you keep this strictly to yourself, Mister Evans, as you promised to do before I revealed the fact.'

Evans came out of his reverie, and stood up.

'Of course, Miss Emerald. You can rely on me! Not a word!'

He bade her goodnight and wandered back over the road to the hotel, leaving Emerald far from happy about her habitual loose mouth.

Back at Heaven's Ridge, Ingrid and Graham wandered in the back way and found the garden empty. Graham suggested a cup of coffee in the kitchen would not go amiss, and they wandered in together, expecting to find Jane there ahead of them, if not Margaret as well. In fact they found neither. The house was silent, and there was no sign of either woman.

'Maybe Jane's gone to lie down,' said Ingrid. 'She often does in the afternoon. She gets very tired stomping around on that leg of hers.'

'What about Margaret? She's usually around,' said Graham, suspiciously.

'She could be anywhere. We could have missed her down the road. She's been doing a bit of paperwork with Evans lately. Maybe she came down the drive as we came up the side way.'

In actual fact they were wrong on both counts. Once Margaret had completed her little talk to Jane in the study, she had decided that the time had come for a certain ritual to be performed on the one destined to carry the family tree downward another branch. That same ritual had been performed in times past on every woman of child-bearing age in the Schuman household. It was called the Blessing!

For a weird family with weird ideas, it wasn't so strange! It was a ritual blessing of the womb that was to carry the new infant into the world. Where it had originated it was hard to tell. But in this particular form it was unique to the descendants of Theodore Schuman.

'I have one further, small request to make,' said Margaret, speaking very tentatively. She hadn't been at one of these blessings since her sister, Helen, had got herself pregnant all those years ago. She had been in the company of her father and. mother at the time, and in truth it had been most distressing to her, and to her sister at the same time. But that was only because they were not prepared beforehand. Jane was pretty broad-minded, so it shouldn't have the same devastating effect on her.

'What's that, aunt?' said Jane, trying to work out how she could smuggle one of those so-called pornographic books back to her room.

'In this family, going back over a hundred years, there has been a ritual carried out called the Blessing, which takes place in a darkened room with the one to be blessed blind-folded. It's like an initiation ceremony, really. The only thing is that once in the room, I will be your guide, and you must obey my instructions down to the letter. All will then be revealed to you, and you will be like an initiate of a secret order, with knowledge that must never be passed on except in a similar ceremony in the future.'

'Will Graham and Ingrid be present?'

'Certainly not! Ingrid was considered too young and immature to be at the last ceremony, which was held in 1975. There was only myself, my father and mother, and my sister Helen – your mother - who was the one to be blessed at the time.'

'It didn't do her much good, did it?' said Jane with a wry smile.

'Helen brought her misfortune on herself. She was ultimately deemed to be unworthy of being trusted with so great a legacy. She was psychologically incapable of adjusting to the concept.'

'Well, you've pretty well lost me,' said Jane. 'Is it going to be painful? These initiations often are, I'm told.'

'Not painful, no! Strange, yes! You will be required to be naked during the ceremony.'

Jane looked around, her attention focused at last.

'Aunt Margaret! I'm truly shocked!'

'I didn't make the rules. I am only the current incumbent, you might say. I merely pass on to you what was passed on to me in lieu of my sister's inability to realize what a great honour she was being accorded.'

'Sounds complicated! I hope I can live up to your expectations. What makes you think I can?'

'Because you're strong, like me! You're irreverent at times, and you often don't take things seriously enough. But that's just a failing of youth. You are about to grow up! I can promise you now that you will leave the ceremony a different person to the one that enters that room. Are you ready?'

'Now's as good a time as any, I suppose. Where do we have to do this?'

'In the room along the passage, the one that's always locked!'

'You mean the one that's supposed to open into the mine shaft of old Theodore? How exciting! I've never seen it!'

'Well, it's not strictly inside that room! However, you'll be privy to all the secrets of this house once you have completed the ceremony, and have been sworn to secrecy.'

'Right,' said Jane. 'When do I strip off?'

'Not until we get inside the room. But you will have to fix the blindfold outside the door. Now, if you will follow me, we will further your education in ways you would never have dreamed.'

Chapter Thirteen

Once Barry Evans had left, Emerald returned inside and began to worry. She shouldn't have said anything! What was wrong with her that she could unthinkingly blurt out the deepest of secrets at the first sign of a friendly face?

Emerald sighed, went into the kitchen and put the kettle on. Then inexplicably she took it off again, and in a fit of agitation brushed her hair, threw on her walking shoes and walked out by the front door. A matter of minutes found her striding along the driveway to Heaven's Ridge. All along the path she was nervously practicing what she would say when she got there, muttering quietly to herself. She needed to see Graham Blood, and warn him. But what if Margaret came to the door? What would she say then?

She got to the front verandah and stood there apprehensively, trying to clear her mind for whatever eventuality. Finally she raised her hand and rapped the knocker on the brass base plate, and listened to it reverberate through the house. For three minutes nothing happened. She was about to knock again when she heard footsteps along the passageway, and to her surprise found herself staring at Graham Blood on the other side of the door. The moment he saw her, he put a finger to his lips, slipped outside and pulled the door shut behind him.

'What on earth are you doing here,' he whispered. 'I thought you were going to wait and see what happened!'

Emerald shook her head, silently, and motioned him off the verandah, away from the doorway. Graham followed her about ten yards to the side of the house, and Emerald spoke.

'I had to see you... I think I've made the most horrible faux pas. I told Barry Evans that you were my cousin!'

Graham slapped his forehead with the palm of his hand.

'What on earth did you go and do that for,' he whispered. 'The guy's out to get me! He thinks I seduced his wife, when in actual fact she came into my room and tried it on. When I came back from having my shower, Evans burst in, and she was lying on the bed, naked. Nothing to do with me! It was all her doing.'

'I believe you, though I know he doesn't. Look, I don't know how it happened. I didn't have time to think it through. It just slipped out, somehow! I know; I'm a big mouth... but what do you do now! If Margaret finds out...'

Graham nodded, grimly. He was under no illusions as to what would happen if Margaret found out.

'Don't you worry about it - just go home. I'll try and get to see you later! We can talk then!'

Emerald reached out and grabbed him by the front of his shirt.

'No - you don't seem to understand. Now that Joan is staying here too, Evans thinks you two are having an affair. You're under the same roof, after all!'

Graham looked at her and frowned.

'What on earth are you talking about? Joan isn't here!'

'She is,' Emerald whispered, urgently. 'She is! Barry brought her up here himself and dropped her off earlier on. I saw them! He didn't know you were here. Now he's fighting mad.'

'Why would she...' Graham began, but stumbled to a halt, because at that moment the front door opened, and Ingrid walked out onto the verandah, She looked around and saw them, almost immediately, standing off to the side.

'Emerald! Oh! What do *you* want?' she said, caught by surprise. 'Margaret doesn't seem to be around at the moment!'

'It's all right, Ingrid, I just had to see Mister Blood here for a few moments. Nothing of importance!'

Emerald turned and hurried off down the drive, casting one long look back over her shoulder at Graham as she went. Ingrid walked over to where Graham was staring after her.

'How is it that you're on speaking terms with our distant cousin, Mister Blood,' she said suspiciously, reverting to her former, more formal mode of address.

Graham ignored the question, and looked suspiciously in his turn at Ingrid.

'Is Joan Evans staying in this house?' he said. 'You'd better tell me, because if you don't, there's going to be all sorts of fireworks.'

'Is that what she came here to tell you,' Ingrid said, sharply. 'The woman's crazy! Of course Joan isn't here... we would have seen her!'

Graham stared at her for a while, to see if he could divine whether or not she was telling the truth.

'If you don't believe me...' Ingrid remarked, angry now at him questioning her veracity. She turned to go inside. Graham reached out and grabbed for her shoulder, and spun her around.

'We have to talk! Go through the house and out into the back garden. I'll meet you behind the sheds.'

Ingrid stared at him sullenly, but nevertheless nodded her agreement and walked back into the house. He followed two minutes later and walked right through and out of the back door.

'Now, what the hell's all this about, Graham? There's something very funny going on here, and it's making me very nervous.'

There was a garden seat against the fence, and Graham walked over and sat down, motioning her to come and sit beside him. She walked over but shook her head, standing in front of him with her arms folded, and looking very defensive.

'I think you know only too well! That little contretemps in the hotel the other night, it was because of me.'

'I thought I'd already indicated to you that I realized you were mixed up in it somewhere. I wasn't going to say anything further about it.'

'Why? Because you thought I was innocent?'

'No! Because it was none of my business! You're a free agent, Graham. I'm not in the habit of pre-judging people on the basis of hearsay, even if my sister is. After all, what is it to me if you were in bed with the woman? I barely know you! At that time, I knew you even less. You were just the odd-job man, and we'd invited you to dinner. So what?'

'That's a very cold, harsh exposition of the facts,' said Graham, suitably chastened. 'I suppose I deserved that! You're right, however... why would it have meant anything to you?'

He was silent for a moment. Then he added:

'For some reason, though, that hurts! Silly, isn't it?'

Ingrid visibly softened, but couldn't quite bring herself to sit next to him

'All right! Tell me what really happened.'

Graham explained how Joan had insinuated herself into his room under false pretences, and then stripped naked while he was in the en suite having a shower. He told her of his total shock when he came out, expecting her to be gone, when Barry Evans burst in through the door.

'In those sorts of situations,' he said, 'it's impossible to try and explain yourself. Even though you're innocent, people tend to go by appearances, and I must admit it must have looked overwhelmingly suspicious from his point of view.'

Ingrid smiled for the first time.

'Poor Mister Evans,' she said. 'It's not the first time, you know! Our Joan has been in a few predicaments over the past few years, usually because she has a tendency to wear her knickers around her ankles.'

She laughed.

'What's this poor Mister Evans?' said Graham, looking suitably chagrined. 'What about poor, maligned Mister Blood?'

'I wouldn't know,' Ingrid replied, flippantly. 'I wouldn't know because I know absolutely nothing about him. Despite being asked repeatedly, he has volunteered no information about his past life, where he comes from, his marital situation, nor his occupation! He might be a serial murderer for all I know, or a night watchmen in a sausage factory. He could be bigamously married to three women, each of whom are benightedly unaware of the existence of the other two. Does that answer your question?'

'All right, I know when I'm beaten,' Graham replied. 'But you're not going to like it! If you want me to, I'll answer all your questions, but I would prefer it if you didn't share the information with your sister, Margaret.'

'Or what?' said Ingrid, suddenly serious.

'Or I might be leaving your establishment a damn sight quicker than I arrived!'

Ingrid shook her head, undecidedly.

'This does not sound good!'

After a few moments thought she reserved the right to do anything at all, depending upon the nature of the revelations. As if in preparation for a shock, she sat down.

'Right! First of all then, I'm not married! No children, either, unless there's the odd bye-blow out there from a misspent youth. Ex-girlfriends there are, in large enough numbers to prove that I'm not gay, but for some reason the right one never came along. I had a doting mother until last year, unfortunately, when the poor dear thing died. Her maiden name was Caroline Hall, her married name Blood, courtesy of my father, Christopher. He in turn was the son of John Blood, who died in a mining accident in the town where I was born... Kalgoorlie! So now you know. Ask me who he was married to and you will have it complete, you who desire to know everything!'

'All right,' said Ingrid. 'Who was John Blood married to?'

Graham hesitated for a moment, then looked Ingrid penetratingly in the eye.

'Elizabeth Schuman,' he said, then sat back and waited.

There was a delay of five seconds, then Ingrid leapt up out of her seat and covered her face with her hands. She spun around to face him.

'No!' she said, as if that one word was enough.

'Yes!' he replied, and watched her shaking her head violently from side to side.

'Oh no, I don't believe it,' she said. 'Not you... not you too! You are, I take it, referring to the Elizabeth Schuman who ran away from home pregnant in the late 1940's, sister of Robert, daughter of Bernard and Barbara Schuman of Heaven's Ridge.'

'That's correct,' said Graham, 'the very one!'

Ingrid took two paces forward and angrily slapped his face. Graham jumped to his feet in shock.

'Hey, what was that for, for God's sake?'

'You're my cousin! And I kissed you, you animal,' she sobbed, suddenly overcome by the weight of the revelation.

'Only your second cousin,' Graham responded, holding his face.

233

'Your father was my first cousin... First cousin! We shared the same grandparents!'

'Yes, but I'm his son, that makes me once removed,' Graham protested.

'It makes you Jane's second cousin, she's all right! You'll be all right with her,' Ingrid cried. She sat down on the seat and wept openly.

'It only counts if you're contemplating having children together,' said Graham, somewhat confused. He hadn't expected a reaction of this nature.

Ingrid cried for a minute, and then calmed down. She became cold and withdrawn, and sat bolt upright and very much apart.

'So you've been here pretty much under false pretences, Mister Blood. That explains why you were so familiar with Emerald... you're her cousin, too. Did she put you up to this?'

'I swear, I never met Emerald before in my life until the night you asked me to dinner. Just after I got thrown out of the hotel, I was standing in the street wondering how I was going to kill an hour or so of time until going up to Heaven's Ridge, when she asked me in. She said she knew me, and I was curious. As it turned out she'd met my grandmother and my father in 1955 when they were in Moonta, on holiday from the west. I must have some mannerism or other that she spotted, that she remembered from my grandmother. The name put the seal on it. She knew who I was! I asked her to keep it to herself until I'd finished at Heaven's Ridge. That's all!'

Ingrid sat silently, twisting her hands together,

'Even if I believed you, that doesn't alter anything, does it? We're cousins, close cousins!'

'We're friends... or I thought we were, Ingrid,' said Graham, gently. 'I only kissed you, I didn't compromise you in any way. Have you never kissed a friend before?'

'Not like that!' said Ingrid. 'No, not like that! You knew the way the wind was blowing, you should have warned me. Now I feel dirty, like I've been a bit of sport to keep you amused. You don't realize how much you've hurt me, Graham Blood! What you've done is unforgiveable!'

She got slowly up out of the seat, and walked purposefully back into the house.

II

Margaret walked Jane along the passageway to the next door, the old oak door that in Jane's entire memory had never been opened. Jane felt apprehensive, and said so.

'I don't know about this, Margaret. This isn't some sort of a joke, is it? I mean, I'm not going to walk in there naked, and suddenly have everyone jump out with balloons yelling *'Happy Birthday Suit'* or something like that.'

Margaret smiled grimly, despite herself.

'I can assure you, Jane, that this ceremony is so utterly secret that even Ingrid doesn't know about it. And she never will, either, if I have any say in it. Once it's over you too will be sworn to secrecy, so you won't be able to tell her anything. You will understand more in about ten minutes. Be patient, girl!'

Margaret fixed a black silk scarf as a blindfold across Jane's eyes, then unlocked the oak door and led her through and into the room. Jane heard the door closed and locked behind her, and stood there, blind in the darkness, listening for any unusual sounds.

'Now I'm going to lead you around a table, and across to an old fireplace, where there are candles on the mantlepiece,' Margaret said. 'I need to light the candles because there is no electric light in this room, and I am as much in the dark as you are at the moment.'

She led Joan by the arm, then stopped, and Joan listened while Margaret struck matches and lit a row of candles. Even behind the blindfold Jane caught a sense of a lightening of the gloom in there.

'That's better,' said Margaret. 'Very well! Now I want you to undress, and drop your clothes on the floor.'

'Are you sure this is necessary,' said Jane. 'For once in my life I'm actually apprehensive about being naked.'

'There is nothing to fear,' Margaret replied.

Jane threw off her dress, then with a slight hesitation took off her underwear and dropped it on the floor. The air was chill in the room, and Jane shivered slightly.

'Now I'm going to lead you over to a large table,' said Margaret, leading her by the arm. 'When we get there I want you to sit up on the table, swivel around to your right and lie flat down on your back.'

Jane did as she was instructed, and lay out flat on the table.

'Now you have to lift your legs, and move down the table towards your feet, keeping your knees bent and feeling with your feet - foot, that is - for the far end of the table. Once you get there, you must lie with your legs apart, your knees bent, then lie back and relax.'

'It's a bit hard to relax under these circumstances,' said Jane. 'I hope this is going to be worth it.'

Once she got into position, Margaret picked up a printed form from the mantlepiece, cleared her throat and by the light of a candle began to read the following.

'We come before you today to bless this womb, that it might become fruitful with your seed which has been passed down to us through many generations of men. Woman is but a gathering house for the seeds of men, that she might extend your generations, and confer divine immortality on your forebears, by keeping alive that part of you which is undying; that familial spirit which runs like a river course through the generations that are not yet come.'

She paused.

'We acknowledge you as the source of our spiritual power, and the source of our material wealth. We give eternal thanks for the wisdom you once displayed in the course of your earthly journey, by providing for your descendants in such a manner that we are still able to sense your presence today, not only in our own physical sensations, but also in the food you bring to our table.'

Margaret halted in her preamble to say in an aside: 'now you must say: *we give thanks, we give thanks; I give myself up humbly to your pleasure!* Say it!'

Stumblingly, Jane repeated the phrases. Margaret continued.

'This humble descendant of your loins now lies naked and unashamed before you, and requests that you bless this womb that will soon swell in parturition, extending your generations towards the future. May the fruit of your loins continue throughout the years to come, and may each new generation reside in true obedience to your wishes at Heaven's Ridge.'

Margaret nudged Jane again. *'We give thanks...'*

'...we give thanks,' Jane intoned. *'I give myself up humbly to your pleasure!'*

'I am now going to place something on you, so don't be frightened.'

Jane heard Margaret moving around to the bottom of the table, then the rustle of material. Shortly she felt an object placed on her vagina and left there, a dead weight.

'God, what is that?' she whispered, horrified. 'It feels like a hand!'

'Be silent, child. Lie quietly and absorb the power!'

Jane lay there and felt her legs begin to shake. The hand was cold and dry, and made no movement whatsoever.

'I acknowledge the great honour that is being accorded to me, and sense your spirit flooding into and filling my womb with your presence. In the coming into and getting out of this sacred receptacle for the seed of man, I will not deny your authority.'

Margaret whispered, 'say: *'I so swear upon my life!'*

Jane repeated: *'I so swear upon my life!'*

'From this moment on I will regard myself as your appointed representative on this earth, and will take upon myself the responsibility of ensuring that the family remains intact and inviolable at Heaven's Ridge. I also swear that if any person should attempt to destroy this harmony, and thus threaten the continuity of your family, then that person shall be my enemy.'

'I so swear upon my life!' said Jane, almost hypnotized by now.

'I also swear that my sacred purpose and knowledge of this blessing, the history of things gone by, the many secrets in which I shall now be

instructed will never be passed along to anyone, until a future time when the following generation is required to replace those that are here now. At that time I will repeat this sacred ceremony, and will pass such knowledge along to the rightful descendant of your line.'

'I so swear, upon my life,' said Jane, now with some force. She sounded as if she really meant it.

'I place my life in the hands of my guide and teacher, your descendant Margaret Schuman, and invest in her the power of life or death over this poor body should I fail in any of these undertakings.'

'I so swear, upon my life,' Jane rasped, her voice now deeper and coarser.

'You may now move back along the table, and sit up,' said Margaret, removing the weight from between Jane's legs.

Jane slid back along the table, sat up and began to remove the blindfold. It took a moment or so for her eyes to accustom themselves to the gloom, but when they did she found herself sitting naked and spread-eagled in front of the figure of a man, who sat quietly at the end of the table. It appeared as if he was looking right at her. She gave out a sudden yelp.

'Don't be afraid. You have been highly honoured. I would like you to meet, for the first time, your great-great-great-grandfather, the honourable Mister Theodore Schuman!'

Jane stared at the man in shock.

'You mean... he's *dead!*' Her jaw dropped, and for a moment she forgot she was naked.

'He's been dead since 1883, Jane! The family have kept him in this room ever since. The port wine pretty well embalmed him, so his skin is a little like leather. Gunther dressed him in his best clothes, and that's what he's still wearing today. He's perfectly intact, and his spirit permeates this house. No doubt you've felt it from time to time, without knowing precisely what it was.'

Jane slid off the table, and began to get dressed.

'I must admit, I've often thought that this place was a little spooky at times.'

She finished dressing then limped around to where Theodore sat motionless in his chair. He sat with his forearms on the table, his big, rough miner's hands in front of him. It had been his left hand that Jane had felt on her body.

'Isn't that incredible,' said Jane, limping around him and viewing him from different angles. 'My own flesh and blood... from a hundred and twenty years ago! That's enough to blow your mind.'

'It is rather awe-inspiring,' Margaret conceded. 'I take it however, that you fully understand now your duties and responsibilities. You must say nothing of this to anyone.'

Jane looked at Margaret with a new reverence.

'Don't worry, Margaret. I'm beginning to see everything in a completely different light. I am beginning to understand, now, why you did what you did to my foot.'

'It was an act of desperation, Jane,' Margaret said, her eyes cast down to the floor. 'But I knew you would understand one day. There have been other things as well, all in the course of complying with this heavy burden that was laid upon me as a young woman. You too will have to shoulder that burden from now on.'

'I'm more than happy to do so, Margaret! You were right... I feel like a new person. To think that you and I are the only ones living that know about Theodore here. It makes me feel humble.'

'It will involve you in making some very difficult decisions at different times in your life, Jane. You must be prepared for that.'

'How come my mother, your sister Helen, didn't carry on the tradition? I would have thought that as she was already pregnant, she would have seen the great honour in it.'

Margaret fell silent for a moment.

'That is one of the secrets that I am now able to divulge to you. Helen was a fretful sort of girl. She just wanted to get away from Heaven's Ridge, and once she met Will Shire, she thought that he was the means by which she could gain her freedom from the family. He was not a very honourable man. He got Helen pregnant, and my father locked Helen in the punishment room each time he returned to the town. He was determined that she wasn't going to ruin her life with a hopeless case like Will Shire. But Helen wouldn't cooperate. Finally, they brought her in here, and with me in attendance performed the ceremony, hoping to bind her by the rules of the blessing. But it didn't work. Helen began to threaten our parents, that she was going to tell the authorities, that she was going to tell Will Shire about Theodore and this strange ceremony they'd made her go through. She was locked back up in the punishment room, but wouldn't relent. Then Will Shire started calling here, and demanding to see Helen. Of course, my father sent him packing, but then he continued to come back again, and caused scenes on the doorstep.'

Margaret paused, rubbed the back of her hand across her forehead.

'It's not as if he wasn't given due warning. When Helen was carrying you, she was still fretful, and had to be constrained. If we'd let her out she would have taken off, nothing was more certain. Will Shire came to the door, demanding to see her and threatening to fetch the police if we didn't give him access to Helen and the child when it was born.'

Jane nodded quietly. She was trying to visualize the scene.

'Anyway, father didn't want the police poking around at any price. So he invited Will inside, and took him up to the large, formal dining room, and sat him down, saying that he would fetch Helen, and they would all hammer it out between them. Well, the long and the short of it is that Will Shire never left the premises again. He's still here, as a matter of fact.'

'Where on earth...'

'You know that little bed of Sweet Williams down the end of the garden? I thought that was a nice touch - my idea, actually. Father thought it was hilarious.'

'So - my father... under the Sweet Williams! God, and I used to joke about that! Sweet William! How poetic!'

'It doesn't distress you, does it, Jane?' said Margaret, observing her, carefully.

Jane tossed her head and smiled.

'No! Not so much as believing that he had just taken off and deserted us. Grandfather Robert must have felt quite threatened.'

'We all did! I took the ceremony a lot more seriously than Helen did, so my father suggested that it would be more appropriate if I continued the tradition, rather than Helen.'

'Did she know what happened to Will Shire?' said Jane, quizzically.

'No, not to my knowledge. She was told three months before the birth that he'd taken off and wasn't coming back. We thought she'd calm down after a while, but after the birth she was as determined as ever to harm the family. My father took me aside, and told me that I would have to deal with the problem. He kept mother inside, brought Helen out from the punishment room, and helped me walk her down the garden. He said that he wanted her to listen to what I had to say, that it might make her change her mind. Then he went back into the house. The moment he'd gone, Helen started to fight me, said she was going to run away. We somehow ended up over by that gateway... there wasn't a gate on it in those days. It was just a spot where we used to sit and admire the view. Anyway, I told her that if she didn't calm down and behave herself, I would be forced to take drastic action. She just laughed at me, so I dragged her over to the edge... she was a lot smaller than I was... and I held her out over the cliff. She said she didn't care, she would see us all in jail for false imprisonment. I think she thought I was bluffing.'

'And you weren't,' said Jane, flatly.

'No! I just let go and she fell head first down the side of the cliff.'

There was the sound of Jane, expelling air from her lungs in a long sigh.

'So that's what happened,' she said, staring at the floor. She repressed a sudden urge to be sick.

'That's exactly what happened! I told father, and he said it was the only option left to us, and not to worry about it. Helen had become a problem, and the problem was solved. He was very pragmatic, my father.'

'What about your mother? What did she say?'

'She was a bit upset, of course. But I remember her saying something about she had known something was wrong with Helen, ever since she was born. She called her the runt of the litter. Of course, my mother wasn't exactly what you would call the sentimental type. She was more down to earth and physical. I'll tell you about her one day.'

Jane took a last look at Theodore.

'Do I get a key to this room from now on.'

'Yes, on the understanding that you are still a novice, and will be taking instruction from me.'

'I understand that,' said Jane, lightly. 'I can't wait to hear all the other gory details!' Her tone was a great deal lighter than her inner turmoil would suggest.

Chapter Fourteen

When Ingrid got up and walked dispiritedly back into the house, she had no clear idea of what she intended to do. The day had begun so well for her, and she had experienced the emotional heights with that kiss beside the old church. Then came the shock revelation that Graham Flood was a cousin after all, and this fact cancelled out all the hopes that had sprung from nowhere into her romantic mind. She walked along to her room, flung herself on the bed, and had a long, self-indulgent cry.

In the back of her mind was a niggling thought that perhaps this cousin thing wasn't as important as she made out. He wasn't strictly a first cousin, after all. He was another generation removed. Did that make it better, or worse? The upside was that he wasn't as closely aligned as she'd first thought. The downside was the twelve years between them, which was just as much an insurmountable barrier as the other.

For the first time, she really envied Jane. She had felt jealousy, of course, for her youth and her undoubted beauty in the past. She had also realized that she wouldn't swap her good leg with

Jane for all the looks in the world. But now she actually envied her, because Jane was definitely a second cousin, and there were no problems with consanguinity in her case.

Ingrid lay face down with her wet eyes buried in the pillow, and felt a wave of hopelessness sweep over her. She felt that her entire life had been inconsequential, and that she was now fated to end it the same way. What, she wondered, had she done in a past existence to merit the punishment she had received this time around? Ingrid was a fatalist, a believer in Karma, and she had often thought that she must have committed some grievous sins in previous lives to account for her misery in this one.

Lying on the bed, it suddenly came to her that they had seen neither Jane nor Margaret since coming back from the church. That was strange! The house was large, but it wasn't large enough to swallow two people up for what seemed like hours. She also wondered about Joan. Why was Graham so insistent that Joan must be in the house? Getting up off the bed, and tidying herself up, she decided to try and find out.

The first place to look was Jane's bedroom. Jane might know if Emerald's story was true or not and if so, where the visitor was. Ingrid sallied along the passageway, pushed Jane's door open and looked in. Jane was lying on her bed, pretty much in the same position that she herself had taken up only a short time ago. She was face down, and her shoulders heaved. When she heard Ingrid come in, she recovered herself quickly, and looked up to see who it was. When she saw it was Ingrid, she fell back again, as if relieved.

'What do you want, Ingrid? I'm not feeling the best at the moment.'

'Whatever's the matter? You've been crying, haven't you?'

'No I haven't,' Jane snapped. 'I'm just miserable and bored and upset. It must be my hormones. Maybe I'm starting the menopause early.'

Ingrid couldn't help smiling. She went over and perched gingerly on the side of the bed.

'I don't think the menopause starts at twenty five, Jane,' she remarked, reassuringly. 'It's only old has-beens like me that get hot flushes and have to kick the covers off in the night.'

Jane rolled over and sat up.

'I'm so confused, Ingrid! I sometimes think that it would be a blessed relief if I wasn't to wake up in the morning. I've even contemplated jumping over the cliff, where my mother... leapt to her death! What do you remember about her, Ingrid? You were her sister, after all. You've never really spoken of her.'

Ingrid smoothed her dress, as she sat wondering what she could tell Jane about her mother.

'Well, for a start, she was the youngest... not by much, but she always seemed a lot younger, if you know what I mean. She had what I'd call an angry personality. She was fretful as a child, used to break my toys if she didn't get what she wanted, She seemed to be always throwing tantrums, and of course mother and father indulged her pretty much when she was small. I suppose it was because she was the youngest, really, because the youngest always seem to get the best end of the deal. The more she demanded, the more they doted on her. Until she got into her teens, at any rate, then she became too much of a handful, and I can remember my father saying to my mother, on many an occasion, 'I don't know what we're going to do about that girl.' In the end she was like an accident waiting to happen, and when she met Will Shire over at the hotel, it finally did. She got herself pregnant.'

Jane looked at Ingrid with interest. She had never been so open before.

'Did you ever meet Will Shire?'

'Oh, I saw him, of course. He used to come to the house and create quite a stink on the doorstep. I used to peek around the curtain, and eavesdrop. It was the only way you ever got to find out about anything around here, because although Margaret was taken into their confidence on some matters, I never was. I was just poor, silly Ingrid to them!'

'Well, don't keep me in suspense. What was he like?' said Jane.

'He was tall... a lot taller than father in actual fact and I think he tried to literally stand over him at times. But father was solid, built like a bull! I think he would have been more than a match for Will Shire. Anyway, he had straight, blonde hair, which is probably where you get it from, because none of us girls were fair. Your mother was so dark that she almost looked like a gypsy. She used to tie her hair up in a scarf, as well, just like the gypsies did come to think of it. Oh,' she said, catching a glance from Jane, 'Will Shire! Well, that's about all I know, really. I never got the chance to talk to him, or anything like that. I do remember, the last day he came to the house, he was in a foul mood, and starting kicking at the front door. He made a terrible racket. I think he was threatening to fetch the police along if we didn't let him see her. So in the end, father let him inside and said he'd go and get Helen, and they could thrash the situation out between them. He took him down to the old formal dining room, the one we never use, left your father there, and came out into the passageway, pulling the door shut behind him. I saw him standing outside the door for about five minutes, and wondered what he was doing. As I walked by, father put his fingers to his lips so that I'd be quiet, then he whispered to me:'

'He thinks I've gone to get Helen, so I'm just letting him cool down for a bit. He's in for a bigger surprise than he realizes!''

'And that was it?' said Jane, incredulously.

'That was it! I don't know what father said to him in the end, but by the time I came back in from making myself scarce in the garden, he was gone.'

Ingrid looked down at her hands, then added quietly: 'I never saw him, nor heard him mentioned again.'

Jane got up off the bed and walked over to the door, pushing it shut.

'When did that bed of Sweet Williams go in, Ingrid? That one down the other end of the garden? Can you remember?'

'That's a funny question. Why do you ask?'

'Morbid curiosity,' said Jane. 'I always thought of it as a memorial to the father I almost had, because of the name, you know! I imagined mother calling him that as a pet name!'

Ingrid looked at Jane suspiciously.

'If I recall correctly, there was nothing there before the baby... you that is... were born. I'm pretty sure of that! The ground may have been turned over, because I recall father talking about growing our own vegetables. But he never actually got around to putting vegies in, and in the end he planted... no! It was Margaret, that's right! She said at tea one night that if he wasn't going to do anything with it, she might as well plant some Sweet Williams. Father just laughed.'

'I vaguely remember him, you know,' Jane mused. 'My grandfather, I mean, not Will Shire. I was about five when he died, five or six, and I remember I was petrified of him. He used to stomp along the passages here with a face like thunder. I remember my grandmother as well. She used to moon around the place as if she was floating on a nylon cloud. She always wore those gossamery things that would billow out as she walked. Funnily enough, I didn't see much of her after father died. She seemed to disappear after a while.'

'She went a bit mental,' said Ingrid. 'Just between you and me, I think that Margaret had to lock her up a lot of the time. Four years after my father died, she passed away too. I used to think she fretted for him, and pined away. But I don't believe that anymore.'

'What do you believe now then,' said Jane, looking at her curiously along the line of her nose.

Ingrid shuffled nervously on the bed, and seemed upset.

'Don't let this go any further... in fact, I shouldn't be saying this, but I think Margaret might have killed her,' she said, quietly.

Jane sat bolt upright and looked at Ingrid in shock and suspicion. What was this? Was it a test? Perhaps Margaret and Ingrid acted in collusion and this was a test to see if Jane would reveal to Ingrid what had happened behind that oak door? After all, Ingrid was supposed to know nothing about the Blessing. Jane had been sworn to silence. She was now a novice, and supposed to be able to control her feelings over dreadful events that had happened before she was even born. Margaret expected her to accept the fact that both her mother and father had been callously murdered with equanimity, coldly and matter-of-factly as if it were the most natural thing in the world.

'That's a terrible thing to say, Ingrid,' Jane remarked, cautiously.

'It may well be, but the more I think about it, the more convinced I am that Margaret knows more about the death of my mother than she lets on. She as good as admitted to me that she'd poisoned father.' Ingrid looked at the closed door, then at Jane, in a mute appeal. She lowered her voice.

'I have this terrible feeling, Jane, that she was with Helen when she fell over the cliff.'

Jane shook her head and got off the bed, distancing herself from Ingrid whom, she thought, was obviously out to trap her into a confidence.

'That's absolute nonsense, Ingrid! My mother committed suicide. She jumped over the cliff of her own free will. She certainly didn't fall...'

'But she may have been pushed,' said Ingrid. 'Don't you see, Jane? She's crazy! If she did murder our parents, and push Helen over the cliff, even if it was all those years ago, who's to say that she won't decide to get rid of you or me one of these days, when the fancy strikes her. She's been getting really angry with me lately over Graham Blood. I really like Graham... in fact I more than like him, Jane. I know it may seem silly to you at my age, but...'

Jane slapped her hands over her ears.

'I don't want to hear this, Ingrid. Please don't confide in me anymore, because I think I'll scream! As far as I'm concerned, Graham's a free agent and he can have anyone he wants. If that means he wants me, even if only to warm his bed for a few days, then I have no intention of turning him down to save your precious feelings. All's fair in love and war, Ingrid, and I'm in need too!'

'Would you feel like that if you suddenly discovered that he was your cousin,' said Ingrid, angrily. She regretted it the moment the words left her mouth.

Jane staggered back in horror.

'What are you talking about? Of course he's not my cousin. Cousins can't have children!'

'They can if they're only second cousins,' said Ingrid, wearily.

The cat was out of the bag now! It was only a matter of time before Margaret was told, and

Graham Blood would be out of their lives once and for all. Ingrid was under no misconceptions about how her sister would receive the news.

'I don't believe you! You just want him for yourself Anyway, if he's my cousin, that must mean that he's your cousin too. So you couldn't have him either!'

'I know,' said Ingrid sadly. There was something in the way she said it that convinced Jane she might be telling the truth.

'How did you find this out?' she said, sharply.

'He told me... I knew there was something going on, because Emerald came to the door a little while ago and I went out there to find them whispering together. I didn't even realize that he knew her. So I was suspicious! We went out, down the garden, and he told me... He's descended from my father's sister, Elizabeth, the one that ran away in the forties.'

'Well, what's he doing here?' said Jane, suddenly feeling the onset of an overwhelming paranoia. If she couldn't trust Ingrid, and she couldn't trust Graham, then who could she trust?

'I didn't think to ask him that,' said Ingrid, taken aback. 'You know, I never thought! I suppose he's hoping to find old Theodore's money. He would have heard the same old family stories that we were told when we were kids, about this fabulous wealth that disappeared when Theodore went to South Africa.'

'Well, I'll be damned,' said Jane. 'And here we are, thinking that all he's interested in is a bit of tail!'

Ingrid screwed up her face at this remark, but forbore to say anything. Jane would be Jane!

'Which reminds me, Jane. He did say something that was a little odd. It seems that Emerald has got it into her head that Joan Evans is hidden somewhere in this house, and that Barry Evans is on the warpath since finding out that Graham's staying here as well. He's drawn the obvious conclusions.'

Jane, who knew nothing about Graham's part in the episode of Joan's naked romp through the bar, needed clarification. Ingrid explained what had happened, and Jane's face changed as she realized the implications.

'So it was him,' she said. 'The old dog! It sounds like he can't keep his hands to himself anywhere else but here.'

'And that's the point, isn't it,' said Ingrid. 'If he was such a lecher as Barry makes out, he would have taken advantage of one of us by now.

Graham told me that it was all Joan's doing, and I believe him.'

'Well, about Joan... I haven't seen her. Where would she be hidden if she were in the house at all?'

The thought struck them both at the same time, and they stared at each other in shock.

'The punishment room!' said Ingrid. 'I wondered why Margaret wanted that key so badly. I thought she might have found out about our little visit there with Graham last night. It was to stop me or anyone else gaining access to it.'

'Surely Evans wouldn't have tamely gone along with that... Punishment!... for Joan!'

'He might have, if the lease of the hotel was a condition of it,' said Ingrid. 'I knew they'd been having talks about the lease! You know what Margaret's like, the moral high ground. Joan's naked foray would have shocked her to the core. She would want the vengeance of the lord visited on her for that!'

'That cage,' said Jane. 'Oh my God! I think Joan's rump is going to get a thrashing!'

They both stared at each other in silence, the Flood draining from their faces.

'What are we going to do about it,' said Ingrid, slowly.

'Nothing! That's what we're going to do... exactly nothing,' said Jane. 'It's nothing to do with us! It's a matter between Barry Evans and Margaret, a private arrangement.'

'And what about Joan? Has it nothing to do with her?'

'She put herself on the spot by slutting around! I believe it's not the first time, Ingrid. She's brought it on herself! If she gets a few stripes across her backside, it's probably no more than she deserves.'

'But what does it say about Margaret?' Ingrid said, shaking her head. 'It's unnatural, this wanting to beat people. I think she's got a sadistic streak in her somewhere.'

'Maybe that's how she gets off,' said Jane, laughing. 'After all... if you don't fuck, and you don't masturbate, what have you got left?'

'Jane!' said Ingrid, holding her ears and blushing furiously. 'I really don't know where you get all this language!'

'Sitting in the bar of the Gold Ridge Hotel,' said Jane. 'If you make yourself inconspicuous in the corner, you can listen to the juiciest topics imaginable. That's where I got my education!'

'If that's education, I don't want it!'

'For a woman of your age, Ingrid, you're incredibly naive. Life isn't all airy-fairy! Romance isn't all roses and sweet innocent kisses, not to men anyway. They have a much more down to earth and realistic expression of love. It's called lust!'

'I'm not sure that I want to be lusted after, Jane.'

'Well it's more exciting than long, mooney sighs in the twilight.'

'If that's the case, what makes you so very different to women like Joan Evans?'

'She has more opportunity than I do, that's all. But she had the misfortune to get caught!' Jane looked at Ingrid with a wicked grin. Her good spirits were beginning to return.

'So you'd expect to be beaten, like Joan?'

'It could be interesting... who knows? I suppose it depends on who's doing the beating.'

Ingrid shook her head in exasperation and got up off the bed. Once conversations like this got under way with Jane, they could lead anywhere. She excused herself, and left the room, pulling the door shut behind her.

II

Barry Evans had other things on his mind. He was out in the shed behind the hotel, dusting down the old 12 gauge double-barreled shotgun that he hadn't used in a couple of years or more. There was a box of cartridges on the shelf, and he grabbed half a dozen and shoved them into his pockets. Then he put the old gun into a vice, and looked around for his grinder.

Since getting back from Emerald's, his mood had gone from red to black. He'd been confused and angry at first when he realized that Graham Flood was staying under the same roof as his wife, then his imagination got to work. He began to get visual images of his wife, locked down in that little cage, and a grim Margaret passing Graham the key in the hallway and telling him to go in there and enjoy himself.

He had no idea what relationship Graham enjoyed with Margaret. Emerald had said that Margaret had no idea that he was their cousin, but he only had her word for that. Maybe Margaret was in on the conspiracy! Perhaps Graham had told her what had happened, how his little affair with Joan had been interrupted, and Margaret had promised to solve the problem, get

Joan under her roof and give him a clear shot at her, without the husband even knowing.

He was inwardly fuming. Margaret had used the lease against him, and he'd had to agree to let Joan go for a month, maybe two. They could be up at Heaven's Ridge this very minute, sipping champagne together or sitting in a bubble bath, making jokes about the cuckold of a husband and how stupidly he had agreed to the deal. He'd fallen for it hook, line and sinker.

Barry's imagination ran riot, and the visions piled themselves one on top of the other. He started up the grinder, picked a point about a foot along the twin barrels and began to cut into them. It only took three minutes and he was through, a sawn-off shotgun, devastating at close range. Now he'd make Graham Flood smile on the other side of his face.

He carried the gun back into the hotel, and hid it behind the bar. Then he emptied his pockets, put the cartridges next to it on the shelf, and looked at the clock. It was six o'clock. The first of his few regulars would be arriving shortly, so he'd have to put it off until after ten o'clock that night. That would probably be better, he reflected. No one would be expecting him, so if there was anything going on he would be liable to catch them with their pants down, so to speak.

Barry sat down on a stool behind the bar, and allowed his mind to fill up with thoughts of revenge.

Chapter Fifteen

When Ingrid left him, to walk disconsolately back into the house, Graham got to his feet, stared after her, and swore. This was not going as planned, not at all. He wandered around to the sheds and thought he'd better make himself scarce for a while. No doubt Margaret was now going to discover his identity, and it would depend on her reaction on what his next move would be.

He took shelter in the second shed, and pulled the door closed behind him. It would do no harm at the moment to disappear. It would give him time to think, time to work out how to make his peace with Ingrid.

The shed he found himself in contained a hotchpotch of general junk, things that had been stored over the years and which was now damp and rat eaten, no good to anybody. There were boxes of Christmas decorations in one corner, and these were in reasonably good condition. They were obviously trotted out year after year and used in the house during the festive season, then returned to storage. Among this pile there was something that took his eye.

It was a box, with a clown sitting loosely on top of it, its long gown designed to drop down and hide the box it sat on. Graham went over and picked it up, then placed it on a bench so he could have a better look at it.

Whatever it was, it was old! Graham took the clown off the top, and saw immediately that it was a Jack-in-the-box, the old jokey type that popped up when you least expected it. But this was different. Surely, the clown fitted inside the box in those things, not over the outside. The unwary would open the lid and a spring would pop the clown up unexpectedly, giving an appropriate shock to the inquisitive. On this one, there wasn't a top as such. The spring mechanism was still there, but it wasn't the weak sort of spring one would usually expect to find in such a toy. In fact, to load this thing would take a considerable amount of force.

The boxes were usually made of wood in these things, but this was some sort of iron plate, incredibly heavy, and very strong. Graham inspected the coil spring, and noted the rust that coated not only the heavy spring, but also the bottom of the box. Not just a light coat of rust, but a heavy layer, as if it had truly been there for years. Alongside the coil was a sort of metal cap, which obviously sat over the top of the spring when it was working, with a concave slot in the middle. The slot obviously had some sort of square-handled stick placed in it that the clown would then sit on.

The mechanism was operated by a kick-plate at the rear of the box. Evidently, a child would sit in front of it, reaching out for the clown, then an adult standing behind the box would give the plate a kick, firing the mechanism and scaring the daylights out of the child as the clown leapt up on the end of the spring. The whole thing was about fifteen inches high.

Graham looked more closely at the rust. It was really unusual, thick and strangely dark for rust. There was an old knife lying on the bench, which Graham picked up to scrape at the bottom of the box. He might as well remove some of the rust and get it working again if he was going to be out there for any length of time.

He'd only been scraping for a minute or so when he realized that the handle of the knife he was using was an unusual shape. It was square instead of wide, and awkward to use. Then something clicked in his mind. He sat the metal cap on top of the spring, then placed the knife, blade up, into the slot. It fitted!

Graham took a step back, and whistled gently to himself, Nasty! The blade protruded out of the top of the box, though obviously, when the spring was compressed, it would sit mainly inside the box.

The more he looked at this contraption, the more uneasy he felt. He took the cap off again, and scraped again at the rust. He was right... he'd thought this was too thick to be rust! Graham rubbed his fingers over it, then rubbed his forefinger and thumb together. No doubt about it! It was old, it was ancient even! But it was blood!

Getting out of the shed unseen, Graham went over to the side gate and made his way along the side track down towards the road. Instead of stepping out where he would be seen, he worked his way through the bushes and round to the back of Emerald's cottage. Entering her little bush garden at the rear, he made his way to the back door, and knocked, quietly. After a few moments he saw Emerald coming tentatively towards the back door, looking worried.

'What on earth...' she began.

'I didn't want to be seen, especially by Evans,' he said, pushing past her into the cottage.

They made their way into her kitchen, and he sat down at the kitchen table. Emerald decided to stand, and she leaned back against the sink.

'A cup of coffee would go down well,' he said, agitated.

'You don't look very happy, Mister Blood. What's happened? Has Ingrid told Margaret about my visit? I know Mister Evans hasn't been up there, because I've been keeping an eye out for him. This really has me worried!'

'Not as worried as I am,' said Graham. 'With Evans after my blood, I'm the prime target. But that's not what I came about. I came to ask you what you knew about Theodore's lost millions.'

Emerald breathed a sigh of relief

'Oh, is that all? I thought that must be the reason for your visit... not this visit, you understand, I meant your overall visit to Heaven's Ridge.'

Graham nodded.

'I grew up with my grandmother telling me all these tales about some fabulous fortune that Theodore had in cash at the time he went to South Africa. It seems it was lost, or disappeared or something. I came here out of curiosity, and obviously, to see if there was any chance of tracing it.'

Emerald laughed as she filled the kettle.

'You and everyone else over the past hundred and twenty years! Even I have my theories!'

'You don't believe it's totally lost, then. Margaret seems to believe that he lost it in a business deal with a man called Barnato at Kimberley.'

'That's right, Barney Barnato! He was quite famous in his time. I actually have a newspaper photostat from a paper in East London, South Africa, reporting that Mr. Barnato was hosting a dinner at which the 'great Australian investor, Theodore Schuman' was to be present. Most of their business wasn't so transparent, however, and never found its way into the papers.'

'So Margaret was right!'

'It depends! What did she tell you?'

'Oh, that Theodore was buying up stolen and illicit diamonds at a discounted rate, for Barnato to salt his mine acquisitions with so he could legalize his so-called finds. They were supposed to be going into partnership together but Theodore died before they got to the paperwork, and Barnato benefited from Theodore's fortune.'

'Not far out,' said Emerald. 'In fact, basically true, as far as it goes. But there were other factors to be taken into consideration. Cecil Rhodes pushed through the Diamond Trade Act at about that time, and that was aimed at those smuggling and stealing diamonds.'

'I don't understand. How would that have affected Theodore?'

'It would have driven him to extreme measures! You see, under the Act, anyone found with an uncut diamond was made to explain how it came into his possession. There was no 'innocence until proven guilty' under that Act. Quite the opposite! It also allowed the company police of De Beers to set up 'Searching Houses', where people could be stripped and searched. In practice, the law was applied more stringently to black workers than to whites, but it was still applied if there was a suspicion that you might be concealing a diamond. The 'Searching Houses' were set up in March 1883, which coincides with the time that Theodore was over there. Actually, he died on the 30th November. He'd been over there ten months.'

'So you think, too, that he spent his money on diamonds that Barnato found in his mines. The money's gone!'

'Oh, the money's gone, sure enough! And by the way, there never were millions! Not then! There was exactly three hundred and fifteen thousand pounds... In 1883 values, that of course equates to many millions of dollars today.'

'But you have no ideas about recovering any of it?'

'I have... but I'll keep them to myself if you don't mind. I will say this! Ask yourself how he died!'

'Well that's something I've never known, and I suppose it would be almost impossible now to find out.'

'It's not what he died of that I'm talking about, it's the manner of his death,' said Emerald, mysteriously. 'And that's all I'm going to say! But if you think about it, I think you'll realize I'm on the right track.'

'If I only knew what track you were on,' Graham sighed. 'I've been thinking of buying myself a shovel, and digging him up,' he said, probingly. But Emerald just looked back at him with a teasing smile, and refused to say anything else.

Dinner at Heaven's Ridge that evening was rather a subdued affair. It was Jane's turn to cook, and as she had difficulty getting around on her foot, Ingrid spent a lot of time in the kitchen with her, helping out. Graham was a little too early to the table, and sat there on his own for a while, looking up each time Ingrid came in, carrying utensils, to see if she would give him a welcoming smile. But she didn't! She kept her eyes studiously averted, and attended to the job in hand. He eventually occupied himself with a book he'd picked off the bookcase in the passageway, called *'A History of the Cape Colony, South Africa.'*

Once he looked up to see Margaret returning from along the passage with a book in her hand that looked suspiciously like a Bible, but she didn't stop, just continued on to her room. When they'd all finally gathered together in the little dining room, they were far from cheerful.

'Good evening, Mister Blood,' Margaret muttered. 'I trust you've kept yourself busy this afternoon.'

'Fair to middling,' Graham replied. 'There have been a few distractions today, but no doubt there'll be plenty to do tomorrow.'

'Plenty to do tonight,' Jane muttered, as if talking to herself.

Ingrid flashed her a dark look, then went conscientiously back to her meal. Graham ignored her, and looked at Margaret.

'We haven't seen much of you today, Margaret. You seem to have been kept busy elsewhere.'

'Sometimes burdens are laid upon us that we cannot ignore, Mister Blood. I am occasionally called upon to help in the instruction of those who reflect extreme cases of moral turpitude, and I do my best to be conscientious in the execution of such duties. Sometimes this is wearying... but we persevere!'

Graham did a mental back flip at this, and looked at Ingrid as if seeking clarification. Ingrid looked briefly at Jane, but neither said a word.

'I've been meaning to ask you, Margaret,' he continued, 'about that memorial stone in the churchyard behind the main street. The one for your great-great-grandfather, Theodore.'

'Yes? What about it,' said Margaret.

'Well, it just seems to me to be a strange sort of inscription for a headstone. It's the sort of thing that one would erect as a memorial if the body was unavailable to be buried. You know, like in a disaster, or a murder case where the body was never found! Are you quite sure that Theodore's body was returned from South Africa?'

Margaret put her knife and fork down. She looked indignant.

'Of course his body was brought back, Mister Blood! It's well documented, as I think I already told you. He was brought back in a barrel of port.'

'And where would that barrel be today?'

This time Margaret looked puzzled.

'What an extraordinary question, Mister Blood! Are you feeling all right? I have no idea, actually. I should imagine it has disintegrated, or been thrown away. It was, as I've said, a hundred and twenty years ago. Is it important?'

'Could be,' said Graham, tucking into the ham.

'I think it's still sitting around the corner, actually,' said Ingrid. 'Or at least, that's what I think it is. You know, Margaret that old water barrel that the overflow goes into from the gutters. I think they used to use it for watering the garden, or as a back-up in cases of drought. I haven't been around that side of the house for ages.'

'Oh, that one,' said Margaret, surprised. 'You know, funnily enough, I'd never even thought about that. It was simply always there when we were growing up, wasn't it Ingrid? It's between the fence and the house on the eastern side. In those days we used it as a hide-and-seek area, because there were bushes to hide behind. It was always very green and lush around that side of the house.'

'Probably because it was shaded in the afternoon,' said Ingrid,

'The barrel always had moss growing on it... I remember now. Isn't that peculiar? I'd never matched the two up in my mind. Why do you ask, Mister Blood? Is there some special significance about the barrel that we should know about?'

'Not really,' said Graham. 'I just wondered what sort of port it could have been that had such an embalming effect on a body. I thought that maybe the maker's name would be inscribed on the barrel.'

'Not that I remember, Ingrid,' said Margaret, looking at her sister. 'Do you?'

'No,' said Ingrid, stealing a look at Graham on her right. 'I don't recall there ever being any printing on it. Mind you, as you said, it was always covered in moss. It might have been there once.'

They were all very silent for a minute or so, then Margaret spoke.

'You know, you sometimes surprise me, Mister Blood. Your mind seems to follow tortuous routes, totally unrelated to the way anyone else thinks. Barrels, of all things!'

'He's almost as devious as the Schumans', isn't he, Margaret,' said Ingrid, coyly. 'You'd think he was one of us!'

Graham stopped eating, and glared at the side of Ingrid's head. She suddenly stopped eating, and began to fan herself vigorously with her hand.

'God, it's hot in here,' she said, 'or is it just me?'

'Just a hot flush,' said Jane, spitefully. 'Menopausal!'

Ingrid looked long and hard at Jane over the top of her plate! Jane was smiling happily to herself, that her jibe had hit the mark.

'You think you've won, don't you,' Ingrid suddenly burst out. 'You think because you're young and attractive, that you're clever with it! Well, sometimes you can be incredibly stupid, Jane.'

'Whoa, ladies,' said Margaret, shocked. 'Now what was that all about, Ingrid? Explain yourself!'

'Jane thinks that our cousin here is going to fall into her lap...'

Ingrid stopped suddenly, and took a deep breath. She looked mortified at the words that had issued from her mouth, as if she'd had no control over them at all.

'Cousin?' Margaret stared at Ingrid, and then at Jane. 'Cousin? Explain yourself! No, on second thoughts, you explain yourself, Mister Blood.'

Graham dropped his fork on the plate with a clatter.

'Well, thank you very much, Ingrid,' he said, pointedly. 'You too, Jane! I have no doubt that you've been exchanging confidences all day. What is it with women that they seem to have a congenital inability to hold their tongues?'

Ingrid looked ashamed, and hid her face in her hands. Jane laughed out loud.

'Oops!' she said. 'Aren't we naughty! If I hadn't been so catty, your secret would have been safe, Mister Blood! Don't blame Ingrid... blame me!'

'I want an explanation, and I want it now,' said Margaret, sternly.

Graham sat back in his seat.

'I have a confession to make, Miss Margaret! I am your cousin, and I came here with the express intention of meeting you all. But for some reason it didn't happen, and when Ingrid here invited me as a stranger to come over and do the odd job, I saw no reason to reveal myself. I apologize!'

'Who are you descended from?' said Margaret, a glint in her eye.

'My grandmother was your father's sister, Elizabeth. You wouldn't remember her. She ran away in the mid-forties... I believe she was pregnant at the time.'

'Yes, I know all about it. My grandmother, Barbara, used to cry herself to sleep in her chair on a regular basis before she died. I think it was very callous of your grandmother to do such a thing. Well... this is a fine to-do! You realize that I would be within my rights to order you from the house.'

Graham looked suitably humble.

'Yes, I realize this. In fact, it would be no more than I deserve! However, against that, if I may say so, I have developed a great respect and affection for you all, and I would hate to see us part on bad terms. Perhaps you could see your way clear to giving me another chance, and letting me stay on for a while. I promise that there will be no more subterfuge.'

Jane and Ingrid looked at each other, and waited with bated breath. Margaret seemed to ignore his plea.

'So, if my working is correct, you would be Jane's second cousin!'

'Yes, that's right. As far as Ingrid and you are concerned, I'm your first cousin, once removed!'

'This changes everything! I think that Ingrid, Jane and I need to discuss the situation in private, Mister Blood. If you don't mind giving us a little time...'

'No, that's fine. I'll just get out of your hair for a while.'

Graham got up from the table and left the room. He wandered along the passage to the rear of the house, taking the torch off the wall by the back door as he went. Then he let himself out into the garden.

Once outside, Graham didn't waste any time. He made his way around to the other side of the house and walked through the small but overgrown plot between the fence and the eastern side of the house. It was very overgrown, and difficult to manoeuvre his way through, but he got there, and there was the barrel, sitting up against the side of the house.

Playing the torch on it, he could see that it had split three quarters of the way down, and now held only a foot of water. It was murky and there were plants growing in the mud at the bottom. Graham pulled on the top hoop, and found he could rock the barrel on its base. With a great effort he pulled it over onto its side, and tipped the water out on the grass. Then he took a long stick and poked around in the mud at the bottom, working it away from the wood, and trying to scrape it out of the barrel. It came out as a pile of sludge, and Graham shone the torch on it as he sifted through it with his fingers.

By this time he was becoming covered with mud, and there was no way that he would be able to explain away his appearance when he went back inside. With a mental shrug, he crawled into the barrel itself, and while playing the torchlight on the bottom, scraped around it with his fingers, paying close attention to the edges. After a minute or so, something caught his eye, and he gave out a great sigh of satisfaction. Further scraping yielded something else, and he picked it up and wiped it on his coat. Then he shone the torch on it, and clearly got the expected result as he let out a little whoop. He crawled out of the barrel, his eyes shining. Making his way back out and around, he made his way inside, and walked along the passage to the dining room, covered in mud and slime. When he appeared in the doorway of the little dining room, the women jumped to their feet in shock.

'What on earth happened to you,' Ingrid exclaimed.

'It looks like you've taken a bit of a tumble,' said Jane.

Margaret just stood there with her mouth open.

Graham threw something onto the table that left a muddy mark on the cloth, then another, then another.

'I was right,' he said. 'I was bloody right!'

Chapter Sixteen

'Why wasn't I told?'

Margaret stared at Ingrid and Jane, her mouth set in a disapproving line.

'We only found out today! It's not as if we've known for any length of time. Then you haven't been around, Margaret. You can't expect to be kept informed if you're not available for hours at a time.'

'I've been very busy today. What about you, Jane?'

'I only just found out from Ingrid myself. It was this afternoon, wasn't it Ingrid, after I returned to my room. You had gone off somewhere, and you didn't reappear until a short time ago.'

'Were you going to tell me?' Margaret looked at them suspiciously.

'I don't know,' said Ingrid. 'I wasn't really going to tell Jane, but it just slipped out. I was trying to work out how I felt myself about the situation, before I confided in anyone else. I'm not a child, Margaret! I shouldn't have to come running to you with everything.'

'If it affects the stability of this household, I should be the first to be told. All decisions affecting us here should be channeled through me!'

'Well I for one think that Graham should be allowed to stay on. Cousin or no cousin he's a nice man, and absolutely no threat to us here.' Ingrid was adamant.

'I don't want to see him turfed out,' said Jane. 'I think he's cute... he amuses me! Let's face it, we get sick of each other's company all the time. He's like a breath of fresh air around here, even if Ingrid has got the hots for him.'

'I must admit, I'm inclined to let him stay on... not permanently of course, but as you say, he's been a diversion for everyone, and his work has certainly perked the place up so far. Ingrid was right there. We did need an odd job man, still do. I suppose we could find enough work to keep him gainfully employed for a month. That's if he *has* a month, of course. He might be on leave from his job.'

'I haven't asked him about that,' said Ingrid. 'I do know that he's not married, and that his mother died last year. His father has been dead for years.'

Margaret looked at her sternly.

'You seem to know quite a bit! I hope you've now got over this infatuation you had for him, now that you know he's your first cousin. That's an impediment!'

'He's once removed,' said Ingrid, rebelliously. 'I've been thinking about it, and it wouldn't matter. I'm too old to have children anyway.'

'But can't you see, it's a moral issue, Ingrid,' said Margaret, a pained look in her eyes.

'Oh, morals morals, you're always on about morals! How come everyone else can have loose morals, and I can't even have one little love affair in my life.'

'What makes you think he wants you, Ingrid,' Jane said, nastily. 'You're not the only bitch in the barnyard. Maybe we could share him,' she said, revelling in the shocked looks of the two sisters. 'I could have him on Mondays, Wednesdays, Fridays and Saturdays, and you could have him on Tuesdays, Thursdays and Sundays.'

'You've even loaded that in your favour,' Ingrid said, with the hint of a smile.

'That's enough, you two. I have a decision to make. If you're going to go on bickering over him like this, then he won't stay. I'll tell him to pack his bags.'

Ingrid and Jane just glared at each other.

'We won't say any more,' said Ingrid. 'We'll just have to leave it up to him.'

'Very well then! He can stay! But if matters start to get out of hand, he will go... sure as eggs are eggs!'

It was at this moment that they heard a shuffle up the passageway, and a dishevelled Graham stood in the doorway grinning from ear to ear.

'I was right,' he said. 'I was bloody right!'

Then he threw something onto the tablecloth, covered in mud. Then two more!

'What on earth are they, and... look at you! How did you get covered in mud?'

Margaret stood back and away from him. There was a certain smell now emanating from his ruined clothes, and it wasn't pretty.

'What do you think they are,' said Graham. 'Here, wash them off!'

He dipped one into Margaret's coffee cup, to her great disgust, then wiped it off on his shirt. It now looked like a piece of rough glass. He held it up to the light, and all sorts of colours began to emanate from it, like a rainbow.

'That's not what I think it is,' said Ingrid, her voice rising. 'It's not, is it?'

'It sure is,' said Graham. 'One uncut diamond from the Kimberley mine in South Africa. Same with the other two on the table! I'm not an expert by any means, but I'd say that big one is all of seven or eight carats. The others, well, they're about four!'

Jane squealed in delight, and for the next two or three minutes there was a constant cacophony of noise as the four of them danced around in circles.

'Good lord,' said Margaret, holding one up to the light. 'Good lord! I can't believe it. Where did you find them?'

'Where I expected to find them,' said Graham, his face flushed with excitement. 'In the bottom of the barrel.'

Jane squealed again.

'So that's where you've been! No wonder you're covered in mud. Are there any more out there?'

'I don't think so, but you can never tell. It's pretty dark. I'll have another look tomorrow.'

'What put you onto that,' said Margaret, recovering her equanimity,

'I just thought it would be worth looking at... anything associated with the old fellow, be it his clothes, or the barrel he was sent back in. We just struck it lucky,' he said, equivocating.

'But there must have been some reason! I mean, dammit, you've just done what people for a hundred and twenty years have failed to do. You've found some of his hoard.'

'Yes, Margaret. But there may be more. I need you to tell me how he died. Believe me, it's important!'

'He was taken ill, went to his bed and died within a couple of days. That's all I know!'

'Did the doctors say what it was?'

'There was some mention of a bleeding ulcer. He was bleeding from both ends, but the family said he'd never had an ulcer in his life. He was as fit as a mallee bull.'

'So basically, he bled to death!'

'That's right! So the story came back to us, anyway.'

'Did they perform an autopsy?'

'Not that I know of. He was a foreigner, in a foreign country. Things were rough in South Africa in those days. I don't suppose they saw any need.'

'Then I think we're in luck. If you've made up your minds about my continued presence here, ladies, I think we may be in luck again, tomorrow!'

Margaret cleared her throat.

'Yes, well... we've decided to give you an opportunity to put things right. You can stay... for the short term, at least!'

Ingrid and Jane looked at each other and smiled in relief.

'I can't believe you've found those diamonds,' said Ingrid, excited now. 'I wonder what they're worth?'

'They're worth more cut than uncut,' said Graham, 'but even rough diamonds this size are worth a fortune.'

'Give us an idea,' said Jane. 'Just a rough estimate.'

'Well, cut stones are worth about $3,000 a carat. So you're looking at, what... $22,000. And by the way, that's U.S. dollars!'

'You're joking,' said Margaret, and fell back into her chair.

Ingrid bounced one on the palm of her hand.

'And they've been sitting in the bottom of a rainwater barrel for a hundred and twenty years.

What do you think happened... did they fall out of his pockets?'

'I don't believe he had any pockets while he was in the barrel,' said Margaret. 'I have an idea the body was submerged in the port, naked.'

'That's my idea, too. He was probably folded in half, his head and his feet pointing up. Which puts me in mind of certain possibilities,' said Graham with a grin. 'Well, ladies... I'm a bit on the nose, so if you don't mind, I'll go and wash this muck off me now, and tidy myself up. When I've done, I'll come out for a coffee. I think I deserve that!'

'I'll make it for you,' said Ingrid, smiling at last.

'So it's true what they say,' Graham laughed, sarcastically. 'Diamonds are a girl's best friend!'

II

Outside, in the dark, a figure was making its way stealthily up the drive. Every now and then it would stop, listen for a moment, then move on. Barry Evans was taking no chances.

When he got to the front verandah, he tried to decide whether it would be better to knock, or just burst in. He conjured up a vision of

Margaret's disapproving glare, and decided against knocking. Although he was armed with a sawn-off shotgun, that was for Blood, not for the ladies of the house. Then, depending on what situation he found his wife in, it might be for her, too. He had two cartridges in place, and six in his pockets.

He reached out and tried the front door. To his surprise, it opened, and he found himself in the front passage. He had only a dim knowledge of the house, and for the life of him couldn't remember which way Margaret had taken Joan to that punishment room of hers. In the light of further events he had come to the conclusion that the room was merely a blind, and that the moment he'd left the house Joan had been let out to join Graham Blood, wherever, in the house. He just had to find them.

He crept along the passageway, keeping the gun down. When he got to the dividing door at the end, he could hear voices. The women were carrying dishes into the kitchen, and laughing amongst themselves. For some reason, their hilarity only made him angrier still. He thought that he might be the butt of their jokes. He waited until he could hear water running in the kitchen, and the clatter of plates, then he judged that they wouldn't be coming out again for a while and passed through the door.

He looked right and left, then decided to take the right-hand passageway, the one forbidden to visitors. He tried the first door, and discovered that Margaret had accidentally left it unlocked. He walked in and looked around, noting that it looked like a study with a considerable library around the walls. Nothing there!

Going out into the passageway again he continued on, and tried the second door. It was locked!

This enraged him! He struggled with the handle, but to no avail. If they were anywhere, carrying on their affair, that's where they would be! He stepped back and took one almighty kick at the door with the flat of his boot but to no effect. It was solid oak, and would take some force to break down.

Not to be beaten by a lousy door, and knowing that his boot had warned them by now, he knew that he needed to get in before the two lovers managed to get their clothes on again. He stood back, raised the gun and pointed it at the lock. There was a mighty explosion as the shotgun blew a hole in the door, pulverizing the lock in the process. Barry kicked it open and charged in. The room was in darkness, the only light being that which filtered in from the passageway. It took a few moments for his eyes to adjust to the darkness, and in the meantime he swung the shotgun around in an arc, covering himself. He'd used one cartridge to blow open the door, there was still one up the spout.

A table began to form in front of his eyes, and as his eyes adjusted, he saw the figure of a man sitting quietly at the end of the table. He didn't move, or attempt to get to his feet, but just sat and apparently stared at the visitor.

'Got you, you bastard! Get on your feet or I'll blow you away! Where's my wife? Joan! Come on out!'

There was the sound of running feet along the passageway.

'Mister Evans!' It was Margaret's voice, shrill and angry beyond belief. She'd heard the shot from the kitchen, and dashed out, panic-stricken, fearing that someone had been shot.

'Don't try to bamboozle me, Miss Margaret. I know they've been together in here, why else would they sit in the dark?'

'There's no one here, Evans! Joan's locked down, and Mister Blood is in the shower!'

'Who's this then?' Evans yelled, waving his gun at Theodore.

'No one! It's just a mannequin. A dummy that we keep sitting in here, wearing some old fashioned clothes.'

Evans walked along to the end of the table and took a better look.

'Hell, this ain't no mannequin! This guy's dead! What the bloody hell's going on here Miss Margaret?'

'You're going to have to get out of here,' Margaret said, in a panic. 'No - don't touch him. I'll fully explain if you'll only come with me!'

She reached out and gingerly took him by the arm.

'I want to see my wife! And I want to see that lecherous bastard that she's been having an affair with behind my back. Now!' he yelled.

Margaret tried to manhandle him back along the passageway, and they passed two white faces peering, frightened, out of the kitchen doorway.

Leading him to the formal dining room, she unlocked the door, and led him inside.

'I'll go and get Joan for you... you'll be able to see that she's quite all right. Then I'll bring Graham along, and you can sit down and talk to him, man to man. But first, give me that gun.'

'No way! I'm hanging on to that. You just bring them both here to me, and I'll sort this out once and for all.'

Margaret led him around to the other side of the long, formal dining table, and ushered him into a chair.

'You just sit there a while, and I'll fetch them both... I promise!'

Evans sat down and put the shotgun flat on the table in front of him.

'Make it snappy,' he said. He wasn't in the mood for equivocation.

Margaret went out of the room, and shut the door behind her. As she did, Ingrid and Graham, newly changed, came running up the passageway.

'Get away you two, for God's sake. He's got a gun, and he's intent on shooting you,' she told Graham.

'We're not going to leave you here on your own. Let me handle it,' said Graham. 'If I can just talk to him, I'll smooth it over.'

'No! It's too late for that. Just let affairs take their course now,' said Margaret.

Graham looked at her speculatively.

'Why are you standing out here in the passage? What are you waiting for?'

'The Lord is doing his work. Everything's in place! He won't threaten us again,' mumbled Margaret, shaking now in a nervous fit.

Graham approached the door.

'Don't, I beg of you,' said Margaret, clearly terrified.

Graham looked at Ingrid, and gave her the nod.

'Take your sister out of harm's way,' he said, and then he opened the door.

Evans bellowed the moment he saw him standing there, and picked up his gun.

'Get off with my wife, would you, you lecherous animal! I'll show you...'

Evans tried to stand up, and to do so threw his boot backwards, under the chair to support his weight. There was a dull thump, a metallic sort of bang and the sound of something sharp slicing through tissue.

Evans stopped dead in his attempt to rise. His face took on a look of intense surprise, and then he slumped down in his chair, and belched blood all over his shirt A moment later his head fell forward and he remained still. Graham started forward in shock. At first he thought that somehow the gun had gone off and Evans had shot himself, but the gun was pointing away from him. He stood, undecided for a moment, then felt an arm on his sleeve.

'Please leave the room,' Margaret said, in a stiff, restrained voice. She was composed now, though very pale, and she seemed quietly determined.

'You know I can't do that, Margaret. This is a terrible state of affairs. What the hell *was* that?'

It was a rhetorical question. Graham knew full well what it was. His mind went back to the box in the shed, with its spring, and evil-looking blade.

Margaret walked around behind Barry's chair, stared down at the back of his head, and looked resigned.

'At least he's out of it now,' she said, as she sat down next to him.

'Don't! For God's sake Margaret, don't! We'll get you help! They'll never convict once they hear about what happened to you as a child, believe me!'

'What would you know, Mister Blood. Are you a clairvoyant or something?'

'I'm pretty good at putting two and two together, Margaret. Plus, Ingrid's told me a few things, and I've worked out the rest from that.'

'Poor Ingrid, she never could keep her mouth shut.'

'You murdered your father, didn't you? You poisoned him at dinner one day. Was that because he abused you, Margaret? He put you in that contraption, that cage, didn't he? Then he would take a strap to you, and then interfere with you while you were helpless. That's it, isn't it?'

'Your perspicacity astounds me, Mister Blood!'

'Then your mother. You murdered her as well! How did you do it, Margaret? You locked her into that contraption, didn't you? Why did you do it, Margaret?'

'She let my father do what he would with me... she didn't protect me! I always swore I'd get her back. I waited my chance, then after father died she became feeble, and I got the upper hand. I locked her in the punishment room! How ironic, eh, Mister Blood?'

'How did you kill her?'

'I rammed a metal rod up inside her and just kept on pushing until she started vomiting blood. She taught me to hate the vagina, Mister Blood! She taught me that it was filthy and evil and only bad things could happen if you played with the vagina. She was right! She died!'

'And what about your sister Helen!'

'That one was easy enough. I pushed her over the cliff! I was acting on the express instructions of my father, however. The sin was his!'

'And Will Shire, Miss Margaret. What happened to Will Shire?'

Jane had finally arrived in the doorway by this time, after limping slowly up the passageway in the direction of the shouting.

'You've just seen what happened to Will Shire, Mister Blood. The same thing that happened to Mister Evans! He sat on one of my father's contraptions, and disembowelled himself. I saw my father waiting outside the room, waiting for him to attempt to get up out of the chair, knowing that the most natural thing in the world when you go to get up is that you bring your foot backwards to support you. What Will Shire didn't know was that underneath his chair was a kick-plate. The moment he kicked it, a twelve inch blade shot up through the seat of his chair into his bowel. No one has ever got out of one of these chairs after that, Mister Blood.'

'I beg you, Miss Margaret, don't do it! We can get you psychiatric help. Even an institution is better than what you're contemplating.'

Margaret looked at him, sternly.

'When your eye offends you, pluck it out, Mister Blood. I have long been offended by everything the good lord manufactured beneath my waist! I'm sorry, Ingrid!'

Margaret stared straight ahead, then kicked back with her foot. There was a metallic bang and a horrible swishing sound that made Margaret sit bolt upright in her seat. She gritted her teeth for a moment, then let out a whimper as blood poured from her mouth and nose, and ran down her neck into her top. Then her head fell back, and she stared sightlessly at the ceiling.

Ingrid screamed, and ran around to her side. Jane collapsed in the doorway, and let out an anguished howl. Graham just stood, helplessly, and shook his head in defeat.

III

It was two thirty the following morning, and the three of them were sitting in the kitchen, still in shock, when Ingrid thought to check the punishment room, to see if Joan was actually there. She went down there with Graham, opened the inner door and found Joan kneeling face down in the cage, her behind covered with livid welts from Margaret's final session of 'tuition'.

She whimpered as they carefully freed her from the cage, then carried her to one of the bedrooms and laid her gently on the bed. Graham left Ingrid to look after her, and administer various creams to soothe the pain. Then he went back to the kitchen.

Jane was still sitting there, gazing steadily at the wall.

'What will you do now, Graham? I suppose you'll call the police?'

'Plenty of time for that! I'll wait now until the morning. No sense in us being up all night, answering questions!'

'You never were very interested in me, were you,' she said.

'You're a very beautiful woman, Jane, and I'm sure that one day you will make some man a wonderful wife.'

'So, do you intend leaving Ingrid behind when you go? That's the usual way of things around here.'

'No, Jane. Strange as it may seem to you, I have a feeling for Ingrid that I never felt for any woman before. It's almost a need to protect her from the vagaries of the world. She's like a fragile little butterfly, and I wouldn't hurt her for the world.'

Jane nodded, tears forming at the corners of her eyes,

'I'm happy for her! But in the meantime, I have responsibilities around here. I made a promise!'

Graham looked at her, wonderingly.

'It's for the best that Margaret is gone, now. Let it all go, Jane!'

She turned to him and smiled, gently.

'I can't! That's just it, I can't!'

Chapter Seventeen

Ingrid arrived back in the kitchen at ten to three in the morning. None of them felt like going to bed, so Ingrid made another cup of coffee while Graham wandered around the house, checking out the damage. He came to the oak door, now blasted beyond recognition, and walked for the first time into the darkened room. Once his eyes adjusted to the light, he noticed the figure of a man sitting at the end of the table, and his jaw dropped.

Lighting one of the candles he found on the mantlepiece, he carried it over and looked at the figure closely. He was wearing a frock coat and a cravat, but his features didn't go with the clothes. He had the rough hands of a miner with broken nails, and callouses. His face had the appearance of a jowly man who hadn't shaved for a week. His side-whiskers were of the period, and were red, but going grey. He had bushy eyebrows, and a rather glum face. His lips were thick and coarse. Graham could almost hear him uttering broken English phrases in a guttural, German dialect.

'Hi, Grandpop,' he said. 'We meet at last.'

When he returned to the kitchen, he looked at Ingrid and shook his head.

'Why didn't you tell me?' he said, looking resigned.

'Tell you what,' she replied. 'I've told you everything!'

'You didn't tell me you kept old Theodore in a closed room, sitting at a table for the past hundred and twenty years.'

Ingrid's jaw fell open in disbelief, and she shook her head in horror.

'That's not true! I've lived here all my life...'

'Ah, but have you ever been in that room past the study?'

'No! That was always kept locked! They said the old shaft was in there, and it was dangerous!'

'Well your great-great-grandfather is in there, and he's waiting to meet you.'

He looked at Jane.

'Are you coming?'

Jane shook her head. 'I met him for the first time earlier on today! I just want to sit awhile and get my head together.'

Graham took Ingrid along the passage, and she followed him reluctantly. Once they were out of earshot of the kitchen Ingrid grabbed his sleeve and asked him to stop. Graham turned at looked at her.

'I didn't tell you everything! I've got a confession to make.'

'What's that,' said Graham.

'I helped Margaret bury Will Shire at the bottom of the garden!'

She looked up at him, a soul in agony, and burst into tears. Graham put his arm round her shoulders, and gave her a squeeze.

'I think I'd already guessed that much. Your father made you do it, didn't he?'

Ingrid nodded, mutely.

'In that case, no blame can attach itself to you. You were only very young at the time.'

Ingrid nodded again, and her shoulders heaved.

'You were an innocent, Ingrid, being manipulated by a dangerous and unscrupulous man, who also happened to be your father. The fact that he had that sort of authority over you meant that you had no choice in the matter. I certainly don't hold it against you, and neither would any other right-thinking individual.'

'Do you mean that?' said Ingrid, drying her eyes.

'Of course I do. We'll make a pact never to mention it again. Jane will never get to hear of it, certainly not from me!'

They continued along the passage, and gingerly peered around the oak door of the mystery room.

'Say hello to your antecedent! Ingrid... Theodore Schuman!'

It took some time for Ingrid to compose herself. She sat on a chair at the side of the table, and stared, and stared.

'How could I have lived here for forty-two years, and not have known he existed,' she said. 'I can't believe it!'

'You can believe it all right,' Graham replied. Then he thought of something. 'Do you mind if I try something out. It's been on my mind all night, and the quicker I get it over, the better. I'd like to do it before the police arrive.'

'All right! Do it, whatever,' she said. Ingrid was still in a daze.

Graham disappeared along the passage, and returned five minutes later with a square looking, box-like affair. He walked around behind the old man, and slid it underneath his chair.

'What on earth are you doing?' said Ingrid. 'That's not one of those...'

'Yes, it certainly is! Your father apparently had a taste for the exotic. This is what you call *Jumping Jack Flash*. But this time, at least, the victim won't feel a thing!'

'Have you gone crazy or something? If you're going to do what I think you're going to do, then I think you need a psychiatrist!'

'Have patience, Ingrid. Think of the barrel! Where do diamonds appear from in a naked man's body?' He looked at her meaningfully. 'I know it's been a rough night, but just have a little patience, and all will be revealed.'

He stood up and slid the box into position with his foot.

'Ready?' he said. Ingrid put her hands over her ears.

Graham gave the box a kick, and the corpse jumped a couple of inches, then settled down on the seat again. Presently, Graham got down on his hands and knees, and turned the box on its side, pulling it out from under the chair. Then he grabbed the handle of the knife and pulled it downwards and out, twisting it as he did so.

Suddenly there was a rattle, as of something falling through onto the floor. Then a stream of small stones began to trickle down, and spread out under the chair. They were all sizes... and they were all diamonds!

'I told you I was right! They were in his bowel, all that time! He swallowed a heap of them! He must have thought he was in danger of being searched, so he swallowed them. They cut his insides to pieces, and he began to bleed internally. That's how he died, Ingrid, smuggling diamonds!'

Ingrid had got up and walked around to where Graham was gathering them up off the floor.

'How many do you think are there, I mean in value.

Graham grinned up at her.

'Oh, a couple of million or so! You're going to be rich, Ingrid. Very rich!'

Ingrid reached over and took the hand of her great-great-grandfather, and kissed it gently.

'Sleep well, old man,' she said, softly. Then she turned and walked slowly from the room.

Graham waited until she had gone, and then explored the room further. There was no window in it. Obviously ultra-violet light would have played havoc with a corpse over that period of time. There was a door, however, hidden away in a far corner. He tried it and found that the wood had swollen in the door-jambs, and it was hard to budge. Putting all his weight against it, however, it finally creaked open, and using a candle to light his way, Graham walked through. He'd only gone six feet when he found himself staring down through a ten-foot hole in the floor. There was a ladder in place, and Graham cautiously turned himself around and mounted it, then slowly descended into what was apparently the original mine of Theodore Schuman. He only had to go down to the first level, and the light played on a scene that would stay in his memory forever. Strewn at the bottom of the ladder were the remains of at least five people, only skeletons now, but still dressed in what remained of the clothes they were wearing when they were murdered.

Graham thought of Robert's devilish boxes, underneath the chairs in the formal dining room. A last supper, then rise to go - *goodbye John!* The body then dumped down the old shaft. Graham shuddered!

Maybe it wasn't just Robert? Perhaps he inherited the taint from his father, and he...

Graham's mind went back to what Emerald had said about Gunther. *'He was definitely loopy for the last ten years of his life.'*

Emerald was right! The family line *was* corrupt, and the sooner it came to an end, the better. Graham climbed back up the ladder a lot faster than he had descended it, got through the door and pulled it shut behind him. The house was an archaic bundle of secrets!

Back in the kitchen, Jane had a request.

'I think you should take Joan back to the hotel. This will be no place for her tomorrow, when the police are swarming all over the house. You two might as well stay there too... it's late! Then tomorrow, call the police from the hotel phone, and come on back up. I'll stay here the night. I'm tired!'

Ingrid went to check on Joan. She was a little delirious, so they agreed that they'd take her back and put her in her own bed. Graham marched on down the hill to fetch Barry's truck, and they loaded Joan into it and drove down to the hotel. Ingrid clung tightly to her bag, which contained all the diamonds, including the ones found in the water barrel.

'I'm not going to let these out of my sight,' she said. 'It's taken a hundred and twenty years to find them and they're not going to be lost again.'

'I do think that you should be generous with your cousin Emerald,' Graham said, after a little thought. 'It was her, after all, that steered me in the right direction. She told me to discover the manner of his death, not just what he died of.'

'She meant the bleeding... it was a dead give-away, wasn't it?'

'Everything's crystal clear in retrospect,' said Graham. 'There were so many people looking for his fortune over the years, but none of them ever picked up on the main clue.'

'In answer to your question, I have every intention of being generous to Emerald, and to Jane. I might even include you, if you're a good boy, and teach me a few things about the raunchier side of life.'

'Ready, and at your service, Madame,' he replied.

They slept that night, entwined together on a bed in one of the hotel's guest rooms.

Jane limped off to lie on her bed, but despite the hour, she couldn't sleep. Echoing in her mind were the words of that oath, the oath she'd sworn to Margaret, and to Theodore. What would happen to him now, she thought. The police would make her bury him. It was so unfair!

'I acknowledge the great honour that is being accorded me!'

Jane rolled over and let her tears soak into the pillow. She couldn't get out of her mind the sound of Margaret's voice, solemnly passing on the duties and responsibilities that she had accepted as a young woman. *'I will regard myself as your appointed representative on this earth, and will take upon myself the responsibility of ensuring that the family remains intact and inviolable at Heaven's Ridge.'*

She thought of Margaret, sitting horribly in that chair, staring sightlessly at the ceiling. Who could imagine what horrors she had been through as a child, to twist and turn her into such a sadistic monster, using the remnants of a religious fervour to disguise her true nature.

'I so swear upon my life!'

She thought of Barry Evans, driven mad with jealousy for a woman who wasn't worth it, and she wondered why she, who had everything except a right foot, could never inspire that sort of love and loyalty in a man.

'I also swear that if any person should attempt to destroy this harmony, and thus threaten the continuity of your family, then that person shall be my enemy...'

And she thought of Ingrid, who had wasted almost three-quarters of her life in a loveless house, but who was now going to live every day like it was forever.

'I sense your spirit, flooding into and filling my womb with your presence.'

She got up out of her bed, and limped along to the back door, reached outside and picked up a tin of kerosine. Then she limped back along the passageway, spilling a liberal amount along the floor as she went.

'I place my life in the hands of my guide and teacher, your descendant Margaret Schuman, and invest in her the power of life or death over this poor body should I fail in any of these undertakings.'

Limping into the old room, its silent sentinel waiting patiently for her to return, she emptied the can across the floor, then limped to the mantlepiece for a candle. Lighting one, she made her way over to the old man.

'Is there room for me there, Gramps?' she said, pushing him backwards into his chair, and arranging herself on his lap. Then she cuddled into his old body, took a last look around, and dropped the candle on the floor.